**'You're cra**

'Yes,' Ricardo a       the woman on s
much more da
stage. As if you would try to deny that passion we both know is there.'

'There's nothing!'

'Do you think passion is only in lovemaking?' Ricardo demanded softly. 'I thought that when I first saw you. You mesmerised me . . .'

'If I've cast a spell on you, then get away!'

**Dear Reader**

This month finds us once again well and truly into winter—season of snow, celebration and new beginnings. And whatever the weather, you can rely on Mills & Boon to bring you sixteen magical new romances to help keep out the cold! We've found you a great selection of stories from all over the world—so let us take you in your mid-winter reading to a Winter Wonderland of love, excitement, and above all, romance!

*The Editor*

**Vanessa Grant** began writing her first romance when she was twelve years old. The novel foundered on page fifty, but Vanessa never forgot the magic of having a love story come to life. Although she went on to become an accountant and a college instructor, she never stopped writing and in 1985 her first Mills & Boon novel was published. Vanessa and her husband live in a log home in the forest on one of British Columbia's Gulf Islands.

**Recent titles by the same author:**

NOTHING LESS THAN LOVE
AFTER ALL THIS TIME
STRANGERS BY DAY

# DANCE OF SEDUCTION

BY

## VANESSA GRANT

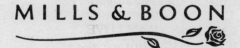

MILLS & BOON LIMITED
ETON HOUSE, 18-24 PARADISE ROAD
RICHMOND, SURREY TW9 1SR

For all the guests at Lynn O'Brien's
marvellous party, where Maria was born

*First published in Great Britain 1993
by Mills & Boon Limited*

© Vanessa Grant 1993

*Australian copyright 1993
Philippine copyright 1994
This edition 1994*

ISBN 0 263 78364 2

*Set in Times Roman 10 on 12 pt.
01-9401-53635 C*

*Made and printed in Great Britain*

# CHAPTER ONE

RICARDO SWAN was facing away from the stage at La Casa del Viento when the music stopped being part of the background. He was speaking to the waiter who had just seated his party, his voice low in deference to the surroundings. While he ordered drinks for his two guests, his mind was occupied with speculation about a time before the Spanish descended on the Americas. A thousand years ago...

La Casa del Viento resided on the first storey of an old colonial mansion. Built of stone in the sixteenth century, La Casa had been designed to endure forever. It had once housed a wealthy Mexican family of pure Spanish descent. For the last thirty years it had been an exclusive club where Mérida's upper class came to dine in an atmosphere of Spanish colonialism. According to Professor Sylviano Talamtes, Ricardo's guest, the stage at La Casa was reserved for Mexico's best performers.

La Gitana, claimed Sylviano, was better than the best.

On the other side of the table Sylviano raised one wrinkled hand as if for silence. The guitarist on stage shifted from background strumming to a rhythm heavy with Spanish haughtiness. Flamenco.

Ricardo would have preferred a simpler evening. His mind was still on the carved surfaces that he'd uncovered from the dust only last week. Mayan inscriptions from the late classic period, but he wanted to take two of the stones to UCLA in California for further study. Permission was tricky, but Ricardo was accustomed to persuading others to his will. First he had called Dr Catherine Jenan in San Francisco. Once she'd agreed to come down to photograph the stones *in situ*, he called Professor Sylviano Talamtes, an elderly but influential archaeologist from the university at Mexico City. If Sylviano could be persuaded that the stones should be dated, his government would certainly agree to let Rick take them.

Ricardo had picked up the elderly Mexican at Mérida's airport, had seen his reaction to the poster advertising La Gitana's appearance at La Casa.

'We'll go there for dinner tonight,' he had suggested, and Sylviano had been enthusiastic.

An accident on the highway just outside Mérida had made them late—a fruit lorry had overturned and spread pineapple everywhere, in chaos. When they finally arrived they found the owner of La Casa had given them a good table to one side of the stage. They were seated with a quiet flourish by a young waiter who looked as if he might be related to the owner.

'...*y tequila*,' concluded Ricardo, nodding to the waiter.

'*Señor*——' The waiter glanced towards the stage. If the *señor* had no objection, he would instruct the kitchen to arrange for Dr Swan's party to be served just after La Gitana's first performance? He himself would bring the beverages at once.

'*Está bien*,' agreed Ricardo.

'It is the same everywhere,' Sylviano murmured as Ricardo sat down at the table with Sylviano and Cathy. 'When she comes on the stage the kitchen holds meals until her song is silent.' The old archaeologist made an expressive gesture. 'Even you, my friend Ricardo. You will dream when La Gitana sings.' He laughed. 'It will not be a dream of carvings on stone.'

Cathy gave the low chuckle that Ricardo had always found so attractive. 'We'll make a bet,' she offered Sylviano. 'Twenty thousand *pesos* says Rick won't succumb to La Gitana. He has all those young students angling after him, but he works them to exhaustion and leaves them all alone.'

'Pale young girls who sunburn.' Sylviano shrugged. 'They have no power. You are the exception, of course, *señora*!' His eyes boldly admired Cathy's blonde fairness. 'Your husband Juan has captured the jewel of the north. But La Gitana—this is a creature of mystique and magic, you understand. She sings the folk songs of Mexico in the style of the Andalusian gypsy—but she is more than a folk singer. She embodies the untouchable quality that is flamenco. No Latin man can resist La Gitana.'

'I'm afraid my Latin blood is firmly under the control of my Canadian ancestors,' Ricardo told Sylviano. On stage the handsome young Latin man was strumming his guitar with increasing passion. As Ricardo watched, the performer stepped into the background.

'Ricardo watches,' said Cathy, her eyes teasing. 'He doesn't get caught.'

Sylviano shrugged. 'I will wager that he cannot watch our gypsy without becoming entangled.' He pulled a bank note from his pocket and placed it on the table. 'Eh, *señora*? Twenty thousand *pesos* on it? Do we have a bet?'

'OK.' Cathy laughed. '*Tenemos una apuesta*. But I warn you, you may lose.'

Ricardo grinned at their nonsense. He wasn't about to offend Sylviano by telling him that he found Latin women too tempestuous, too emotional. The blonde woman seated with them was more to Ricardo's taste. Unfortunately, Catherine Jenan de Corsica belonged to another man.

There had been a time when he and Cathy's Peruvian husband had faced off like enemies. A time when Ricardo had hoped he might win Cathy for his wife. She was exactly the woman he had always wanted. Intelligent, cool and rational, and as fascinated by the mysteries of history as he was. Restful, with none of the uncomfortable Latin mystique of his mother's people.

Marriage should be rational. Ricardo had no intention of needing a woman badly enough to lose sight of reason. He'd seen it happen to others. To his mother. To Juan Corsica Perez, the Peruvian who had pursued Dr Catherine Jenan across more than a decade in time and the length of a continent.

'If I do lose,' said Cathy in an undertone, 'Jack would love the chance to send *you* a telegram.' On stage, the Mexican man was building up to the flourish of words that would bring La Gitana on to the stage.

'Tell him,' murmured Ricardo, 'that it will happen when this mansion is dust like the ruins of the Mayans.' Despite the fact that he spent much of his time in Mexico and in Ecuador, when it came time to love he would do it gringo-style: with reason and cool blood.

'A telegram?' asked Sylviano.

'When Jack and I were *novios*——' Cathy made a gesture and added a Spanish word that indicated Ricardo had done a service for the couple.

On the stage a lean, handsome Mexican took the microphone and began to speak.

'I don't know who he is,' said Sylviano. 'Her father introduced her performance when I saw her perform in Mexico City last winter. I didn't see this man. The guitarist—the handsome young man on her right—I believe he was playing the instrument in Mexico City. Ah—Ricardo, now!'

A flash of red caught his gaze. Her dress. A seductive swirl of heavy skirts. Satin? Whatever the fabric was, it seemed alive. All heavy swirling red and the incredible black of her hair sweeping her shoulders and back. A waterfall of black hair cascading over shoulders of impossible soft ivory.

Her head lifted high with the haughty sensuous notes of the guitar.

She froze in a pose that seduced motion.

The guitar breathed sharp, shallow rhythm.

Something caught in his throat.

She moved.

Her hair...a riot of passion on the ivory of her shoulders. Long red skirts shifting rhythmically against endless woman's legs. For a moment it seemed that she was motionless, only her gown moving. The rhythm of flamenco swept through the caress of that heavy red skirt. Rhythm hinting at the shape of the woman's body concealed...obscured from view by fabric...her neck slender and long...past her throat to the place where folds of red satin concealed the details of her flesh from a man's eyes.

When she moved...

He told himself there was nothing. He could see nothing. Only fabric and the rhythm of the dance. The movement was in the fabric, the shape hinted in the motion. But his mind lost reason in the rhythm. Spanish rhythm. Gypsy rhythm. The mystery that was woman. Passion. Dark red lips parted...the sound of a woman's husky voice...eyes...her eyes might be any colour at this distance but the woman herself was moving as if the sounds from the guitar were the echo of her lover...the husky notes of her voice an invitation no man could mistake.

The woman on the stage was filled with sultry motion...passion unconfined...La Gitana. She had no name on the posters. La Gitana...the gypsy. She needed no name.

She moved and the image went straight to a man's gut. She sang and the sound tangled in his pulse. The guitar shifted tempo and the pulse in his veins accelerated and she was there with it, her hips swinging in a parody that was from bewitching dances around old camp-fires in Spain.

Then the woman's voice fell silent. The guitar raced. The gypsy's body moved with controlled passion in the old rhythm. From somewhere there came castanets and the guitar slipped away. The rhythm of her arms pulsed out on two levels. Again his mind tried to impose logic on her magic. The castanets. *Hembra* and *marcho*. He had studied the chestnut-wood instruments once in Mexico city. The female rhythm would be *hembra* in her right hand, the larger *marcho* in her left, snapping out the male part of the rhythm.

Male. Female. Her arms and hands creating the beat that flowed everywhere in her. The music of passion promised. Passion controlled by a thread of the will in a woman whose every breath was seduction.

When the tension was too great, the audience breathless and in pain from their silence, the beat of the male rhythm grew strong, dancing with the female for control. Then the guitar and there was a crash of sound and her heels on the stage and suddenly silence echoing and her head thrown down, then back in a pose that was triumph as the applause came.

Ricardo gripped his glass and fought the insane need to go up there and forcibly prevent her leaving.

She wasn't leaving. Not yet. Moving to the microphone. Slow movement, and no woman could walk like that on the streets without a pack of men following after her. Slow movement and his eyes locked on her. Part of him saw her strategy. The slow, seductive approach to the microphone gave her time to collect her breath after the fast passion of the dance. She was going to sing.

The guitar began to echo the slow pulse of a gypsy camp-fire. The red fabric swung slowly against her...slow sound...slow passion slid into his veins to replace the violence of her dance.

Cathy's hand gripped his arm.

He jerked his head around. Cathy. Blonde curly hair. Frowning lips. Her face was fuller than it had been when he first met her. She was different. Softer. Glowing with the love she had found. Radiant with the knowledge of the life she carried. Juan Corsica's child. Juan Corsica's wife.

'What did you say, Cathy?' On the stage the woman moved and he could not stop himself from twisting his head to watch her.

'There isn't a man in this room with normal blood-pressure since that woman came on stage.' Cathy's laugh was breathless, as if she too were affected. 'What about my twenty thousand *pesos*?'

Ricardo made himself look away from the stage. Away from the woman with no name. He focused on Cathy. Short wavy blonde hair. Outspoken, sensible—if one discounted her passion for the man she had married. Exactly the sort of woman he would one day make his wife.

'Don't worry,' he said. 'Your money is safe. I'm afraid Sylviano is going to be the one in the poor-house.'

Sylviano flew home from Mérida airport the next afternoon. Cathy stayed at the dig, explaining that she would leave at siesta-time because she was expecting a call from Juan. He was in Paris on business and Cathy was hoping he would return to Mérida by the end of the week.

Ricardo waved Sylviano off with a box of priceless Mayan artefacts, bound for the university. Then he returned—not to the excavation, but to La Casa del Viento. The manager greeted him as if he knew why he had returned.

He ate before she came on stage. Eating without tasting, listening to the music and waiting for the change in the sound of the guitar. The change that meant she was coming on stage. He almost left when he had eaten, because this was insanity.

La Gitana . . . at last she came.

The long red folds of her skirt swept out and back against her body. She tilted her head back in a haughty challenge. Her lips parted and the song was a pulse that made his fingers curl in on themselves. She was like an illness on him.

He'd been too long working in the Yucatán. He would fly down to Quito to visit his mother and his sisters, attend to business there. Or better yet, New York and he could look up Sarah, a historian who had taught at UCLA until two years ago. He hadn't seen her in two years, but . . .

Sarah was tall and cool and blonde, not unlike Cathy in appearance. The sort of woman he liked. Quiet. Intelligent. Rational.

La Gitana...

A woman *learned* to move that way. She must have studied the seduction and the heat of movement. Learned it wherever she learned flamenco. It had to be make-up and costumes and a fantastic vein of sultry heat that stopped the heart of every man she danced for. She would dance for her lovers too. Stage stuff.

He could not fight the conviction that the fantasy became real when she moved. She was real...she *was* the dance. She had a beautiful voice, a husky contralto. The words...he could not make his mind attach meaning to the words. And when she danced...raw sensuality imprisoned by the dance...if she were dancing in his arms...alone by candlelight...each item of those swirling gypsy clothes thrown off as the music heated...

He watched and a part of him fought the spell. She was too obvious, too much the sensual female. He liked women with brains and not nearly so much in the way of sultry curves. He wouldn't come again.

Perhaps he would dream of her as he had last night, but he would not come to watch her again.

The first song moved into a dance as the music went wild. La Gitana. Her arms and her body. She twisted and there were no words, only sensations and the dance in his veins. She came out of a spin with the red skirt full and the image of her long beautiful legs on his mind as if he were not quite certain he'd seen. He had to stop his hand reaching out towards her.

He would have sworn she sang the last song to him, although he knew the audience was nothing to her, unless she had a lover here, watching. He jerked around to look and they were all watching her. All wishing...or did one of those men know that she would come to him later...to her lover?

Perhaps the young guitarist was her lover. He must be about her age. She would be in her mid-twenties, or perhaps older with the signs concealed by make-up. In his experience young women in their twenties were not particularly sensual. When a woman reached her thirties...

Her eyes were half closed, her throat exposed. Her voice was whispering song and love for the man who came to her in secret. The guitarist was echoing her emotions, but softly enough to leave room for her voice. La Gitana was far too much woman for such a young man as the guitarist. She was created for love...for secret liaisons...passion in the heat of a Mérida afternoon. She was a woman a man might pay any price to possess. The gifts a wealthy man gave when there would never be more than gifts. He knew how it went. He'd spent enough summers in Ecuador watching his older cousins when he was a boy. And that one year when he was eighteen...Elisa.

She would laugh that husky sound and her lover's jewels would adorn her beautiful throat long after the lover was gone... La Gitana... He would give her diamonds.

No, not diamonds. Rubies to echo the red gown she wore so seductively. He would put a gold bracelet around her wrist. Rubies around her throat.

For as long as it lasted he would be her only lover. He would make sure there was no other. He would——

Madness! He had to get out of here. Fly south to check on the new general manager of the Ecuadorean mining operation, north to the gold mine in Canada, then on to academic sanity in his office at UCLA...anywhere at all where there were no seductive gypsies.

La Gitana turned her head.

He could have sworn that her eyes locked on his. A trick of the lighting made her eyes flash as if with a green fire. A woman who exuded love and mystery on command. Her voice, the movements of her body...when that thin mask of control was gone from her the music of her loving...

La Gitana would be his lover before he left Mérida.

On Friday night La Casa del Viento was packed with everyone from the mayor of Mérida to the owner of Mexico's largest recording studio. Maria didn't see the tall dark man on Friday. She didn't look for him.

Not exactly.

Saturday, standing behind the curtain just off stage as she waited for Miguel to introduce her first number, Maria watched her mother pull the edge of the curtain aside.

'Is *he* here?' Maria asked in a whisper, her hands clenching in the folds of the red dress.

Her mother let the curtain fall. 'Everyone is here,' she whispered as she adjusted Maria's costume before the first song. '*Todo el mundo*. They have come to see La Gitana.'

Maria moved the edge of the curtain. She recognised the mayor of Mérida with a party of guests. Beyond the mayor was a large party of wealthy gringos. Beyond them—— The lighting prevented her seeing further.

'Is *he* there?'

Her mother nodded. 'The same table. You have a conquest there, *chica*.'

'He makes me nervous.'

The same table. It was a special table, reserved for parties of distinction. Friends of the management or government officials. For it to be occupied by a man alone when La Gitana was performing...

For the first time in years, Maria wished she could be anywhere but where she was: standing in the wings, about to go on stage at one of Mérida's most elegant nightclubs. When she moved on stage she would see nothing but the lights. Normally she preferred the lights to the intimacy of a smaller performance. Making eye-contact with the men in her audience often made her nervous, although once the music started nothing else mattered. Normally...

The first time she noticed him had been Tuesday. Miguel liked to match the lighting to the mood of her music and when she finished the last words of the Lisbon song the imitation moonlight flowed over her. The audience came clear in front of her as the lights faded. He was there.

It happened again when she sang the wanderer song. Unnerving, because she was facing *his way* as the lights went down. He was staring back at her. The club broke into thunderous applause but he did not move in the slightest.

He stared at her. As if...

'I don't like the lights,' she told Miguel that night. 'It unnerves me when they go down into that blue moonlight effect...I end up staring at the audience.'

Miguel had shrugged her protest off. 'The effect is great. It brings the house down and if you're nervous it doesn't show. Don't worry, *chica*. Let your big brother look after the lighting.'

Wednesday she was staring straight ahead with her head thrown back and her eyes half closed as she came out of the wanderer song. Then the lights went down and in those seconds while she was blinded by the old brightness she imagined he was there, but alone this time. Staring at her.

She gasped when her vision came clear and it was him...as if he'd forced through the barrier between audience and performer. The barrier that made it possible for her to be La Gitana.

'Flowers again,' murmured her mother in Spanish. 'He sends flowers again to your dressing-room.'

'Maybe it's not him sending them.' Flowers from the audience were wonderful and fragrant. She loved them. But flowers from the man who had stared at her in artificial moonlight all this last week?

'His flowers, yes,' said her mother. 'I asked the owner. He said——'

'No! Don't tell me about him!' Her mother would have asked questions. The owner of the club would know the answers. The best table in the house and he'd been there alone the last three days.

'*Chica*, did you see the flowers?'

'Yes.' Maria's voice was husky. 'Send them to the orphanage. He makes me nervous.'

'You?' Her mother laughed. 'They all love you. They send flowers and ask you to dine. If he is important Miguel will invite him to dinner next week.'

'No!' Not him! Not the tall man with the frowning face. Watching her.

'You will smile for him. He will remember the smile from La Gitana across a candlelit table in Mérida. If he is not important...' Maria's mother shrugged. 'Even a bull cannot get past Miguel. He is nothing. Only an admirer.'

Maria could hear Miguel's voice from on stage, the strumming music from Emilio's guitar.

'...La Gitana!' announced Miguel.

As the audience called her name, Emilio's bass guitar beat out the rhythm that was her theme. Maria felt her body begin to move with the music as she stepped on to the stage. The applause was a roar in her ears. She liked it that way, the audience part of the music . . . not individuals clapping and calling out to her. The lights making them unreal. For just a moment as she saw the mass of shapes beyond the lights she felt a shaft of fear, that *he* was out there. Watching. Not clapping and not smiling, but seeing something the rest could not see. But music was throbbing and her body took over, flooding out her fear and setting her hips swinging with the rhythm so that her full red skirts swirled and she forgot the man who had watched all week.

Miguel stepped back with a flourish and Maria was alone with the bright lights and the music, a microphone in one hand. Emilio's guitar raced breathlessly. She swept her hand back in the gesture that brought the guitar in Emilio's hands to soft rhythm.

It was a love song. Breathless music and throaty words in Spanish. She let her voice go husky and hot with the music, breathing of sultry tropical nights and a man who haunted her. He was a dream man. Faceless in her mind, walking towards her on the clean sand of her own beaches and never close enough to be more than the dream. It was a gypsy song. The love was a sad love . . . a lost love. With the music throbbing deeply Maria tilted her head back to expose the long curve of her throat . . . to let the resonance of her voice fill and call out on the night air.

She could feel the faint scent of tropical flowers on the night. The air cooling from the heat of a tropical day. She twisted her body instinctively and her skirts moved with the rhythm of her pulse. Her lover's spirit

touched her and the song was everything, magic and reality and seductive patterns of light and sound and sense.
She could feel it all, the scents of the night and the magic
of the music, the rhythm of her own body reflected in
the motion of her skirts and the sensation of her long
hair moving over her bare shoulders as if it too were
alive and in love.

She was the gypsy. This was her place, buried in the
music and the dance. She *was* the music as her voice
took the soft song to a climax of love and pain. Then
the beat of Emilio's guitar turned hard as it filled with
wild loneliness. As she breathed the last of the song the
lights would be fading, and she kept her eyes closed until
she had taken the beat of the guitar and whirled away
from the microphone.

She came close enough to Emilio in her movement to
close her hands on the castanets he held out to her. She
slipped the castanets on to her hands and stamped her
foot and the passion of life came full in her voice and
her body...a woman's song of protest and love.

The lights softened as she sung the last notes.

He was there. Watching her.

One song flowed into the next...and the next...until
she was whirling off the stage in a sweep of gauzy skirts
and into her mother's waiting arms. She pushed away
from her mother and went back to where Miguel was
working the controls for the lights.

'Don't put the lights down like that when I'm doing
the Lisbon love song,' she said sharply. 'If you must
play with them like that, please *don't* do it while I'm
singing Lisbon.'

'*Chica*, it's a fabulous effect, you in that red dress and
the moonlight while you're singing that song.'

She sucked in a ragged breath. 'I don't like it.'

Miguel turned a dial at the panel that controlled sound and lighting. He was a handsome man with a serious frowning face. 'Why not?' he asked, frowning up at her.

Because the stranger was watching, making it seem as if she had no choice but to sing those love words to him.

'Forget it,' she muttered. '*No es importante.*' She could not explain to him. All her life he had been her best friend, her protector and adviser. But he would never understand the uneasy feeling crawling up her back when she locked eyes with the frowning man at that table.

# CHAPTER TWO

'Two hours,' murmured Maria in Spanish. 'Get me out of here in two hours, Emilio, or I'll be dead when we rehearse tomorrow.'

Her younger brother bent down to take her arm as she stepped out of the limousine. The driver bowed them towards the *casa*. Maria kept a light hold on Emilio's arm as they went up the broad marble stairs.

'Have I ever failed you?' Emilio was grinning, not taking this as seriously as Miguel would have. Dressed for formality as he had been when they performed, Emilio was every young girl's dream of a romantic Latin hero. Before the evening ended, there would be some young beauty staring up into his eyes with breathless hope.

'La Gitana,' announced Emilio in a formal whisper, 'will be——' he lifted his wrist and pretended to look at his watch in the dark '—safely in her bed in two hours and five minutes.'

'I'll hold you to that,' warned Maria.

Emilio might try, but it wasn't realistic. Maria could hear the sounds of the party within when the maid opened the door to the *casa*. Laughter. Music. If they got back to the hotel before four in the morning it would be a minor miracle.

A courtly man with greying hair came hurrying towards them. 'La Gitana!'

Emilio stepped back to leave Maria in the limelight. She moved forward, smiling, tiredness suppressed. The

21

maid took her wrap. Her host smiled enthusiastically and moved theatrically as he urged her through a massive carved archway towards the noise.

It was a performance. Maria glanced at Emilio, a silent message to stay at her side. To the elderly man, she said, 'Your home is beautiful Señor Descanso.' It was true, the entrance hall a vast area of beautiful marble and generous curves.

He made a gesture of deprecation. 'You honour it, *señorita*! And Señor Concerta,' he added, nodding to Emilio who had fallen behind them to make way for a woman wearing a black lace headdress. 'Your guitar is a magic carpet for the gypsy music.'

Señor Descanso was speaking in English as he had a year ago when Maria first met him. He spoke English with a distinct accent, but seemed determined to prove his fluency. He held out both hands to Emilio. The men exchanged the traditional greeting that made them seem more than vague acquaintances. Maria saw amusement in Emilio's eyes as Señor Descanso turned back to Maria.

'*Señorita*, I have followed your career with such interest since we met in Mexico City last year.'

'*Gracias, señor.*'

Miguel had done the talking for her at that meeting last year. In Mexico women didn't negotiate if there was a man to speak for them, and in any case Miguel was an astute manager. Better than her father had been. The president of the record company that produced her records had introduced Enrico Descanso to Miguel and Maria with a deference that made sense when Miguel later discovered that Descanso owned thirty per cent of the company.

Which made the invitation to join a few friends at his Mérida *casa* a command performance for La Gitana and her guitarist. Otherwise they'd both have chosen to stay in their hotel tonight, to rest in preparation for the carnival fiesta tomorrow. So they had come, both in costume for the occasion. Maria was wearing a long green dress of satin crocheted in an intricate pattern above the waist, its full heavy skirt swaying slightly as she moved.

'You must meet my friends,' urged Señor Descanso.

Maria's eyes followed as he gestured towards the room through the broad marble archway. Reality distorted for a second and she had the illusion that she had stopped moving.

'No,' she whispered, but mercifully there was no sound.

Emilio touched her arm. '*Chica*? *Está bien*?'

'Stick close,' she whispered.

Señor Descanso's hand was pressing her upper arm, urging her closer. She *was* moving closer... tried to look somewhere else. The room was a blur of people around the man in their path. People close to him, too, but her steps seemed to take her straight towards him and in another step... or two... she would break free and run. Out of here. Away.

He was tall. She hadn't realised how tall from on stage. She'd seen broad shoulders when she looked down on him through Miguel's artificial moonlight. Too broad. Eyes too far away for details, just an impression of heavy brows and shadows around dark eyes. No smile. That was all she'd known. Dark hair. Big shoulders. Frowning face and the impression of power. Watching her.

Brown eyes. She could see them clearly now. Too close, and she moved another step with all the sounds of the party far away and hollow. Señor Descanso and Emilio on either side of her like guards taking her to... to him.

His eyes pinned her and she had to force herself to keep moving. One step after another. No expression on his face. A trap.

Run!

She couldn't run. Insane to think it was necessary. Emilio was right beside her. She was in the middle of a crowd of wealthy Mexicans. She was perfectly safe.

She rested her hand on Emilio's arm.

'Quite the spread,' Emilio murmured in her ear.

The man's eyes narrowed. Maria had an impression of anger. She gripped her brother's arm more tightly. Heavy dark brows over those penetrating brown eyes. Black hair with a determined wave that showed strongly despite the conservative cut. She had assumed he was Latin when she saw him in the club, but now she wasn't certain. For one thing, he was too tall. His face was all hard lines and frowning lips as it watched her. A face with the look of easy laughter too... but no laughter when he looked at her. As if he'd taken one look and known something terrible about her.

It wasn't sensible, but she wished she didn't have to take that last step towards him. Whenever the lights went down and she looked at him from the stage she'd seen that frown. Those eyes. The one man who had refused to stay on the other side of the lights.

He frightened her.

Illusion. Miguel's trick with the lights. It wouldn't happen again. Tonight had been her last night at La Casa del Viento. Next week she was scheduled to give performances for the carnival crowd. Then she would be gone. She'd never see him again. He was no more a danger than any of a hundred men who had watched her. Men whose eyes took liberties. She just had to get through tonight and she would be safe from him.

She tried to look away.

'Dr Ricardo Swan,' her host murmured. He gestured Maria forward, introducing her with a deliberate flourish. 'La Gitana! Our gypsy.'

Dr Swan bowed slightly, his smile ironic. *'Exquisita,'* he murmured.

She curtsied in acknowledgment of his compliment. His watchful eyes seemed to give the movement a significance it should not have had. He reached for her hand.

She didn't want to let him touch her but there was no choice.

Slowly, he lifted her fingers to his lips. Eyes on hers. She could not look away.

'Are you actually gypsy?' His voice was deep, low-pitched enough that he would be bass in song. His Spanish had an accent she did not recognise. His lips brushed the back of her hand so lightly she wasn't sure of the contact. Just the shiver that crawled down her spine as she pulled her hand away.

'Gypsy is a state of mind.' Her voice felt uncomfortably husky.

'And this is the magician on the guitar,' added Señor Descanso. 'Emilio Concerta.'

Dr Swan's eyes narrowed. Emilio gave a slight, formal bow. Her brother's smooth formality seemed weak beside the powerful confidence of Dr Swan. She didn't like his kind of man. Too aware of his power.

His eyes told her what he wanted.

He had sent roses to her dressing-room. Red roses. Later he would dance with her if he could. Perhaps trap her in a corner and make suggestions in a voice too low for the respectable women to overhear.

Ricardo Swan. His name was half Latin and half *norte americano*. He must be wealthy. She and Emilio were the celebrities. The other guests were here by virtue of wealth and ancestry. She lifted her head slightly and met his eyes. She recognised what she saw there. It wasn't the first time she'd seen it. Not the first powerful man to make her glad of her brothers close by. Maria wasn't naïve; she knew what a wealthy and highly educated man of her own culture would expect to gain from pursuit of La Gitana.

Well, let him pursue. It would get him nowhere. With Miguel and Emilio between her and men like *him*, she had no reason to be nervous. No reason to think of the look in a man's eyes as anything more than part of the applause at the end of a performance.

His gaze drifted down the satin of her gown. 'There is much of Andalusia in your dancing,' he said in Spanish. 'But it is not *flamenco puro*?'

'If you can find pure flamenco,' she said quietly. 'You won't find two scholars to agree that it's pure.'

He shifted smoothly to English. 'Are you suggesting that your popular interpretation is as valid as anyone else's?'

He *was* testing her. Checking out her linguistics! Or her education! And smiling as if he mocked her.

'Flamenco can't be understood outside its historical context,' she answered in English. 'Folk music and dance are living entities.' She lifted her gaze directly to his. A mistake, she realised as their gazes locked. She couldn't seem to look away.

'And La Gitana? Who is she?'

She shrugged the question away. 'It's a pleasure to have met you, Doctor.' What sort of doctor? She shivered at the thought of being alone with him in an examining room.

'Ricardo,' he said softly.

'*Gracias* for the flowers,' she said. She did not repeat his name. 'You did send flowers? Roses?'

'And I will again,' he promised. '*Hasta luego, señorita.*'

His eyes told her that he fully intended much more intimate contact than could be had in a party at Señor Descanso's *casa*. She must need a holiday when the look in a man's eyes got to her like this. Either that or there was something more dangerous about this man than the others.

Beside her, Emilio asked, 'You are a doctor of medicine?'

Maria breathed again. Those brown eyes had made her forget where she was. A quiet party in a Mérida mansion and her brother was at her side, questioning Dr Swan in the politest way, but he was her escort and this was a very formal gathering.

'An archaeologist,' said Dr Swan.

An archaeologist? Here in the Yucatán he would be a student of the Maya? Good God! He was more than that! Power in that face. Frightening power, the kind of man who knew he would win.

Señor Descanso was speaking and Maria turned thankfully away from the man who made her so uneasy.

'Señora Catalina Jenan de Corsica,' her host said with a flourish, bringing Maria towards a blonde woman dressed in a loose flowing gown of satin.

The woman from Dr Swan's table. That first night, a group of three and *she* had surely been one of them. She looked a gringa but she was talking to Maria in warm fluent Spanish. For a moment Maria forgot that Emilio's voice was talking close by, and *his* was answering.

'You live in Mérida, *señora*?' she asked the blonde woman.

'No. In San Francisco. I'm just waiting for my husband to join me here.' Her eyes flickered over the crowded room as if she thought the husband might turn up at any moment. 'And do call me Cathy,' she added with a warm smile for Maria.

Her husband. Maria's gaze flickered to Dr Swan. That first night at the club, he had been laughing with this woman. Maria had watched them in the moments before she went on stage.

Señor Descanso introduced Maria to another couple and she was able to move away from that group, Emilio at her side a moment later. Then her brother disappeared, but it no longer mattered. By that time Maria was safely in a group of four other women standing near the drinks bar. A maid handed her a drink. In the corner two men were playing guitar lightly. Background. Not dancing, although there would be dancing later. Maria would be asked to sing. Singing for her supper, she thought wryly, but Señor Descanso had asked in a manner that did leave her room to refuse. She'd agreed, of course.

She would eat very lightly, drink little. The singing would be after the late supper her host had mentioned, so she would be starving by the time she got away. Before that happened, she knew that Dr Swan would come to her.

She glanced back to the place where he'd been but he was not there. She wished again that Miguel had come with her tonight. Her older brother was skilled at deflecting the men who inevitably thought they could pursue the image they saw on stage. He was tall and heavy-set, a legacy of their American grandmother. He also had a way of looking very serious when he referred to her as his sister. With Miguel around, no one bothered her.

A beautiful young woman from Mexico City began to question Maria about the origins of the Lisbon love song. The plain young girl at her side asked if Maria had a *novio*.

'I'm too busy,' said Maria. They all laughed. It was impossible, said one, that any woman would be too busy for men.

'The men are mostly married here,' said the one named Consuelo. Her eyes slid past Maria.

Unwillingly, Maria turned her head to look. He was standing perhaps ten feet away in deep conversation with the blonde gringa woman named Cathy.

'He's mine,' said Consuelo. The other women laughed.

'She wishes,' said the woman from Mexico City. 'He belongs to the Maya in the ruins. Or perhaps he wishes to have *la rubia*—the blonde woman. Last summer we all thought they would be *novios*.'

'Who is she?'

'The wife of Juan Corsica. He is Peruvian. Very wealthy and very...' She made an expressive gesture indicating that the gringa's husband was very handsome. 'She is *americana*. But married and you understand, *very* married. Her husband comes next week and as you can see from her dress, she is *embarazada*.' She made a gesture to indicate the swelling of a baby. 'She is also a doctor like Señor Swan—for the Mayan ruins. And he— he is from everywhere, that one. Consuelo is not the only one who would like to think she interests him.'

The women laughed as if it were a familiar joke.

'Perhaps he wants La Gitana,' suggested Consuelo. 'If I had your looks...' She made a gesture and the laughter came again. Somehow Maria managed to smile in answer to their warm teasing. 'He is of a very important family... very *macho* but not for...' Another expressive gesture.

Consuelo shrugged. 'Perhaps it is true that he loves *la rubia*, or perhaps there is a woman he is promised to in Ecuador.'

'He's from Ecuador?' She didn't want to know the answer, hadn't meant to ask.

Consuelo said, 'His mother is, but he travels. You understand in any case he is one who always goes away. To California. To Ecuador. Other places—who knows?' She shrugged.

'Consuelo dreams,' said the beauty. 'She has been haunting those ruins whenever he comes, sad when he goes away.'

The music increased in intensity. Consuelo looked at someone over Maria's shoulder. When Maria turned, it was only Señor Descanso. Her heart settled back to normal.

'La Gitana,' he murmured. 'Would you dance with me? It is only the waltz. I cannot dance flamenco, you understand. But if you would do me the honour.'

She smiled and went with him to where the marble floor was cleared for dancing. She saw that they would be the first to dance. He was her host and he was beginning the dancing by taking the floor with his famous guest. Part of the show.

She smiled and moved into his arms. He wanted to please her and he did not hold her too closely or ask questions to probe. In any case she supposed he had access to most of the information that the studio had about her. Her public history was no secret.

'Do you like Mérida, *señorita*?'

'Yes, especially during *carnaval*.'

'Really?' He laughed and steered her around a pillar in their path. 'You are the performer everyone will come to see this year. Is that not work for you? Surely not play?'

Something in his smile reminded her of her own uncle. 'During the day,' she confessed, 'I play hooky.'

'Hooky? An American phrase?'

'Yes. It's slang. It means *hacer novillos*.'

'Like a child hiding from school?' He nodded understanding. 'I do the same in my home outside Mexico City. I pretend to be a poor man so that I can share simple pleasures with my family. What do you do when you run away from La Gitana?'

'Only what everyone else does during carnival. Go on the streets. Visit the artisans' booths. Buy a *burrito* and eat it on the street. Watch the children who have come for the magic.'

He shook his head. 'Your picture is everywhere on posters in Mérida. There will be a riot when they recognise you.'

'No one recognises me. I shall be *incógnita*.'

He laughed with pleasure. 'Would you have dinner with my wife and me when you are in Mexico City next month?'

'May I bring my brother?'

'Yes, of course. My wife is British, you know, but her father——' He smiled as if offering her a present. 'Her father was a gypsy from Andalusia. She'll enjoy you tremendously.'

Maria shook her head. 'I am only playing the part of La Gitana. Your wife will see through me at once.'

'You play the part perhaps better than you know. Ah, here he comes——'

'Who?'

'Who else?' he said gently, smiling down at her as if she were his daughter. 'He watched the door until you came. And then he watched *you*.'

She could not see him, but her breath packed up in her chest. Not yet! She needed a minute . . . even seconds to be ready for him. She needed the mask of the gypsy and in this moment she could feel only her own nervous awareness of him as a man.

'Shall I surrender this dance to him, *señorita*? He is after all a——'

She shook her head desperately. 'I—I have to find Emilio.'

'He's dancing with my niece. I'm sure my niece is thrilled to be dancing with La Gitana's guitarist. She will be in the stores tomorrow buying all your tapes. Where did you learn to speak English so well? Ah——'

She was as tall as Señor Descanso but she had to look up to the trap of Ricardo Swan's gaze. He was standing behind her partner, touching his shoulder.

'*Con permiso*?' The question was only a polite formality.

Señor Descanso sighed and smiled at Maria. '*Señorita*, I will remember this dance forever. You make an old man young again.'

Ricardo Swan took his place. Took Maria into his arms. Passed from one man to the other, from safety to danger, she thought wildly, as if . . .

It was a dance. Only a dance. A difficult performance, that was all.

He was a far more demanding dancer than the relaxed Señor Descanso. His body had a natural sense of music that invited her to slip into the dance.

'Where did you learn to speak English?' he asked as he guided her steps in the rhythm of the music. His hand rested on her back in such a way that the tips of his fingers made contact with the bare skin above the back of her gown.

She held herself as far from him as she could. She couldn't breathe. She could feel the stiffness growing inside her.

'*Dónde?*' he asked in Spanish, reminding her of his question.

She swallowed twice to find her voice. 'I grew up speaking both English and Spanish at home.'

'Why.'

'My father was half American.'

He brought her closer. She stared at his shoulder, uncomfortably conscious of his height and the strong breadth of his shoulders.

'Was he?' He had shifted to English again and she wondered if he was trying to confuse her. 'I understand that your father introduced your act when you gave a concert in Mexico City last year?'

'*Sí,*' she agreed. She fixed her eyes on her own hand as it rested in his. He was not gripping her hand. They lay together. Two hands. She willed hers to be still. Not to pull away. She must not let him see how his touch disturbed her. 'My father died last year,' she said tonelessly.

'I'm sorry.'

Emilio was sweeping Señor Descanso's niece past with a flourish of energy. The girl looked flushed and half in love. Emilio himself looked more affected than usual considering that the girl was not blonde. Like many of his countrymen, Emilio was fascinated by fair women.

'He's far too young for you,' said the voice above her head.

'What?' she gasped, then she made the mistake of staring straight up into his eyes. He was too tall. Too big entirely. She didn't like dancing with men who made her look up.

He nodded towards the couple now dancing around the marble pillar. 'Your guitarist. Your escort. That girl is more his age, and I'm sure you can do better.'

She pulled back. His arm at her back prevented escape. That and the fact that they were being watched by half the guests. She wanted to run but she knew the other half of the guests would stare soon enough if La Gitana ran from a man on the dance-floor.

'But not your host,' he said softly, as if this were an intimate conversation. 'You'll not conquer him despite his soft words of praise for La Gitana. He's quite ridiculously in love with his wife. What *is* your name? I refuse to call you "gypsy".'

She shifted and realised from his eyes that she'd tried to shrug his touch off. They were dancing, his embrace only the contact between two partners. She felt the heat in her face. The compression in her chest grew tighter. She had to get away from him.

'Any more advice?' she asked. 'You've recommended I leave Emilio...but not pin my dreams on Señor Descanso?'

'I've said too much, but you have that effect on a man.' His hand pressed her closer as he steered her around the pillar Emilio had swept the young Descanso girl behind. 'I'm sure you're aware of what you do to the men you perform for.'

'What exactly is that?' she demanded in a voice that felt like ice. She tipped her head back and stared up at his face. *Dios*! If only Miguel were here! Emilio would never be able to face down this man. The arrogance in his eyes was the confidence that came from knowing his own power.

'We'll leave that conversation for some other time,' he murmured with a slow smile. She wanted to pull her eyes away but she could not seem to do anything except stare up and up, and she was turning dizzy.

'You have incredible eyes.' His voice was husky. A lover's voice.

She gulped and jerked her head. Staring at his shoulders now. He was wearing a light brown suit jacket. The eyes were dangerous. Maybe because she had to look up to see them. Up and up and he made her feel small. Too small. Too helpless.

'Where were you educated?'

She shook her head.

The music drifted to silence and she stepped back from him.

'No,' he said quietly, retaining his hold on her hand and her back. 'I claim another dance.'

She had a terrifying vision of pulling away from him, running away around that marble pillar. Him chasing and he would catch her with no effort. The music began again and he began to move with her.

'Where were you educated?' he asked again.

'Where were you?' she retorted. He was closer now, the dance-floor more crowded. She could feel his shoulders. He was holding her so that her breasts brushed against him as they moved. It was hot in the room. Terribly hot! Stifling...

'Montreal,' he said. She felt him shrug. 'Quito, then Harvard and UCLA.'

Three countries? Canada and Ecuador and the States. Her lips parted on questions but she did not ask. Every nuance of his voice told her what he wanted. He ate girls like her for breakfast and spat them back out. He was dangerous. She'd seen in his eyes that he had the sickness. He wanted the image from on stage. La Gitana. The gypsy was a fantasy woman, but he was the sort of man who got what he wanted.

He wanted her.

He used the hand that was holding hers to press against her chin, forcing it up. 'Your turn,' he said. 'Capsule history?'

'Chihuahua,' she whispered. 'Los Angeles. Mexico City.'

'Los Angeles? When?'

She wasn't going to answer. She knew she should be playing the role but she couldn't. Not with him. He made her feel as if he were under the skin of her pretence.

'You're not exactly what I expected,' he said.

'What did you expect?' She felt herself stiffen and his hands still on her. She realised with panic that they were dancing in the open window that led out to a balcony. She wasn't going out there with him! She wanted to get away but if she moved she would pull too hard. If she said too many words she might scream instead of whispering. She felt brittle and his hands could easily break her. Her eyes found his and she was glad when the anger came. Better than the panic. 'Perhaps you expected me to be more...amenable?' she suggested.

He was moving and she was stepping back to stop his getting closer. But it was through that window. Outside on to that balcony. Cool air but he was between her and the open window that led to the other guests.

He had her out on the balcony. Alone! How had she let him do that? Didn't she know better? Her breathing was harsh and the fear was very real.

'You expected I might be interested in performing flamenco for you?' she demanded.

'More than flamenco.' His voice was dead serious. His eyes wanted her.

'More than flamenco,' she echoed. The room, the other guests were only there—but a scream would freeze in her throat. 'How do you plan to persuade me to give you...more?' She tilted her head back so that her eyes could be only angry slits looking at him. 'I'm expensive, you understand.' Anger let her gaze slide down over him as if in assessment. 'I've no idea of your price-range. Roses, I know. You've sent roses. What comes after the roses?' She threw her head back and stared at his face.

He was angry, his face all hard lines and she could see both men in him. Ricardo Swan. The Latin in him was furious. If it weren't for the cold gringo keeping the anger confined she would be regretting her outspokenness.

She pulled away and his touch was gone but his eyes were on her and this was no way to get rid of a man. She knew it was asking for trouble talking as she had...but he'd caught her off balance, getting his hands on her on the dance-floor when she wasn't expecting it and now she was stuck with his tall broad shoulders a wall between her and the safety of the dance hall.

She managed a laugh. It sounded the sort of amusement that might have come from a real gypsy. Suddenly she was on stage again and he was at least on the other side of the light, the inches of air between them a barrier of some kind. She was La Gitana, an Andalusian gypsy flaming with scorn at the rich Spaniard who lusted after her.

That was what it was. Lust.

'Rubies?' she suggested. 'Gold? Does the price you're able to pay stretch to diamonds?'

'Only if you're very good,' he said softly.

'I'm very expensive,' she said. And she laughed that laugh, the one that went with the haughty passion of flamenco. Then she leaned forward and said clearly, 'And I don't want *you*. Diamonds would not be enough.'

She pulled her skirts aside with a violent gesture as old as the gypsies she imitated. Her skin crawled as she came beside him because she couldn't see him now and he was going to reach for her, catch her with one strong hand. She'd felt the strength of the hand that had held hers. He hadn't used that strength against her but he could, easily. And what could she do?

Scream? And explain it how afterwards? Artistic temperament, perhaps? There was no other excuse. He hadn't touched her except in the formality of dance. Behind her now. He was behind her.

She hurried inside, into the light. She made her lips shape a smile as she made her way through the dancers. Then mercifully Emilio was there in front of her without the niece in his arms.

'Dance with me,' she said, going into her brother's arms. 'And for God's sake *don't* let anyone cut in!'

## CH...

MARIA stopped at a booth... *carnaval* ... the music and... from the country to be sold... sation. Too many people. Too... chaotic sound to be real. She rea... a soft creation of patchwork leather. Th... ne would be on stage, but this afternoon sh... escape and watch the magic. Her fingers caressed the softness of the leather.

'Special for you, *señorita*,' said the tradesman's voice at her side. 'Only ten dollars.'

He had spoken to her in English and quoted the price in dollars, proof that her costume today was effective. She was playing the part of a *gringa turista*. *Incógnita*, she had told Señor Descanso, and it was true that no one recognised her once she put on American jeans and pulled her hair back into a plain ponytail.

'No, thank you.' She spoke in English. She smiled and the artisan smiled back.

In the next booth Maria found an elderly woman dressed in a colourless shawl attending a display of painted ceramic dishes. Maria touched the gentle shape of a rose petal on a serving bowl. None of the goods was priced. Maria knew the price would be flexible. More for a tourist, less for a local.

'Five dollars,' offered the woman.

She shook her head and moved on. She had no urge to buy. Only to look and touch and breathe in the feel

touched a deep red woven
of colourful clothing. Then she
of a treat she remembered and her head
gaze searching the crowd.

e! A stainless steel cart at the corner bearing the
message *'Hot Dogs exquisitos!'* The top of the cart was
a steel cooking surface, steaming hot. A boy of about
fourteen was moving sizzling frankfurters on the surface
with a spatula. Maria made her way to the cart and pulled
out two coins.

'One, please,' she told the boy. Earlier she had decided that today she would be a tourist who spoke no
Spanish at all, not even the obligatory *'por favor'*.

*'Con todo?'* The boy shifted a frankfurter on to the
sizzling centre of the cooking surface.

'Yes,' she agreed. 'With everything.' She knew that
much Spanish, she decided. She suspected that the boy
spoke little English.

'I've been watching you,' a man's voice said. 'Following you since the leather display.' When his hand
touched her shoulder she gasped.

She spun around to face him. Ricardo Swan, staring
at her with open curiosity. For long seconds she could
say nothing. Then she remembered that she was an
American tourist today. *Incógnita*. She decided that she
was an American of English extraction, irritated and
politely haughty at this stranger.

'Pardon me?'

He shook his head, his smile growing. 'Maria,' he said
softly. 'Maria Concerta.'

She shook her head in denial.

His fingers tightened on her shoulder. 'You may as
well talk to me. You will in the end, so why play
this game?'

She shook her head again, slowly.

'*Una más*!' he instructed the hot dog boy. His hand was still on her upper arm and she thought that his grip would tighten the instant she tried to pull away. She knew well enough how cruelly strong a man's touch could be.

'Let go of me.' Her voice was tight with the effort it took to repress the scream.

'Not yet, I think. We'll browse the other displays while we eat, shall we?'

'No,' she ground out. 'We won't.'

He smiled as if her denial meant nothing.

She stepped back. Her breath came again when she realised that he *had* released his grip on her. The boy held out the two hot dogs towards them. Ricardo Swan took both hot dogs. Behind him a man and a woman in Mardi Gras costumes walked past in a crowd of men costumed in formal suits.

'I want to be alone, Dr Swan.' She would run, she decided. Surely he wouldn't chase her? Not in this crowd filled with police. She would turn away and melt into the people.

He touched her waist and guided her to the edge of the pavement. She pulled against his touch but he didn't seem to notice her straining against his guiding hand. When he stopped to look down at her she had the panicked conviction that he intended to take her into his arms. Surely he wouldn't? Not here with the hot dog boy watching and two husky Mexicans hurrying through the crowd towards them, moving fast as if to run down anyone in their path. As the fast-moving men came abreast Ricardo Swan shifted slightly to put himself between them and Maria. Protecting her.

'I want you to leave me alone.' She said it clearly, staring at his chin.

'You're not alone.' The squareness of his chin echoed the lowered brows above his deep-set eyes. The face of a man who got his way. 'I'm with you now.'

'But I want——'

He shook his head. He held out her hot dog. She saw her hand reach out to accept it even as she told herself to turn away. She felt anger in her throat but the words had stopped. Then his hand was on her arm just above the elbow and he was guiding her through the crowd, shifting his own body to make a barrier when others crushed too close.

When they reached the leather display, the artisan came towards them with fresh enthusiasm. Ricardo gestured towards the patchwork handbag she had admired earlier.

'No!' she protested. 'You were watching me here earlier?' Scary, because she'd been so pleased with herself. Grinning at the tradesman and floating from stall to stall in her own version of carnival. She'd had no sense of danger.

He was pulling out money.

'I won't accept it from you,' she warned.

'Not today, perhaps, but one day.'

The tradesman was wrapping his gift in response to Ricardo's command.

'You paid too much,' she muttered, and the harsh lines of his face shifted into amusement.

'A man doesn't bargain when he's buying a gift for a beautiful and mysterious woman.'

He'd watched her all week from that table at La Casa del Viento. The gypsy. Gypsies were mysterious. That was why he was following. He wanted to trap the mystery he thought he saw when she danced.

She moved away from the leather goods. Past the ceramics. Stood still staring at a display of silver jewellry and deliberately took a bite of her hot dog.

'Silver is too cold for you.' He was standing behind her. His voice was quiet, but she heard it clearly and shivered. She turned her head and had to look up to see his eyes. Brown eyes with gold flames. He held the parcel containing the handbag under one arm as he took a bite of his hot dog. She watched him swallow, watched the sensual pleasure that flowed over his expression. Around them a group of young girls flowed past, holding hands to keep track of each other in the crowd.

'I didn't come here to be La Gitana.'

'No, I can see that.' He was studying her.

'Then leave me alone.' She looked away from him and concentrated on the last of her hot dog. He brushed his hands with a napkin and offered it to her. She brushed her own fingers and then he took the soiled paper away from her.

His eyes seemed to be staking a claim on her. Her heart began thumping.

'I'm leaving! I'm going back to my hotel now.' Hotel. The word became tangled with a vision of a bed in her mind...and in his eyes. She gulped and backed away from him. That was what he wanted. Sex. He'd watched her from the beginning, wanting...

'You perform at eight tonight,' he reminded her. His full lips curved into a slight smile. 'It's only four now. You weren't planning to go back yet, were you?'

She told herself to run but her legs did not move. She was insane, frightened by a quiet man in broad daylight in a crowd. 'Last night,' she asked unsteadily, 'when I sang...were you watching me?'

'Of course.'

She'd stood there with the microphone in her hand and Emilio's guitar sounding around her. She'd sung with the gypsy freedom that made her forget there were men in the audience. Ricardo watching.

A predator who wanted to make Maria Concerta his prey.

'I want to be alone. I told you that. I don't want——'

'Yes,' he agreed. 'You told me, but you lied. Your eyes meet mine and we both know it is meant.'

'No!' On Señor Descanso's balcony he'd been staking a claim. A sexual claim although he hadn't touched her. He touched her arm now, urging her aside from the crowd. His head bent close to hers and his voice made her shiver.

'You tremble when I touch you in the dance. You must know I felt you respond to my touch. Who are you, Maria? Why are you in costume today?'

'In costume?' Her fingers spread on the denim covering her thighs.

'Jeans and that cotton blouse that pretends to hide your body. When you stand motionless you are hidden, but when you begin to walk—then La Gitana reveals herself. And your eyes——'

Somehow his touch froze her ability to pull back. They were perhaps thirty metres from the square where there would be dancing later. The musicians were tuning their instruments and playing scraps of songs.

'If you want La Gitana, come to the performance to-night.' She shivered as she said it, suddenly afraid that she would never be able to dance again without his eyes watching. 'La Gitana lives only on stage.'

'I'm not sure that's true.' He took a fold of her blouse and rubbed the fabric thoughtfully between thumb and

forefinger. 'Of course you know how seductive the
mystery is? The gypsy veils herself in American unisex
clothing...hair tied back...face bare of make-up.' His
gaze touched the places he described. Her hair. Her face.
'No perfume. No seductive clothing. Yet the gypsy es-
capes when you walk. Why did you come on to the streets
in this costume?'

She was shaking her head back and forth, denying his
images yet trapped by them. He was dangerous. She got
tangled in his words so deeply that she felt her body
trying to move. Yet she knew that with his eyes on her
the slightest movement of her body would have a seductive meaning. She stared into his hard face with the
deep brown eyes and almost believed the wild thought
that she moved and breathed to draw him to her.

'Why did you come in disguise?'

She shuddered. 'To enjoy *carnaval* alone.'

'Enjoy it with me.'

She must have shaken her head, because he echoed
the motion.

'Yes, Maria. You can't escape. You've made yourself
a mystery. I never could walk away from a mystery.'

Of course she could escape. That policeman on the
corner and the crowd all around. In a minute she would
go. 'Is that why you became an archaeologist?' she asked.

'Perhaps,' he agreed. 'The eternal need to uncover
what history has hidden.'

'Don't you take it seriously?'

'I take the Maya seriously. They made their mark on
this world we stand in.' He shrugged and his gaze swept
the people around them. 'My own need to know—that's
simple curiosity. A sort of irritation that history hides
the details from me in dust.'

He took her arm and urged her away from the musicians. She breathed in the scent of *burritos* from a stand they were passing, glanced up and saw a half-smile on his face. It had been so long since she'd been alone with a man that she had lost her perspective. His hand was on her arm and she could feel his heat against her shoulder. She didn't like the contact, but he was in no position to hurt her in the midst of this crowd.

'You've been coming down here for years, haven't you, Dr Swan?'

'Four years.'

'Have you uncovered all the Mayan secrets?'

'Only some.' Again she caught that intriguing hint of self-mockery. 'Call me Ricardo, Maria. You're not one of my students.'

'Will you mind leaving?' His brows went up in a question and she flushed. 'Someone mentioned that your excavation was almost finished.'

He shrugged and she realised that she was looking at the gringo part of him, a man who would not be ruled by passions or needs. On the balcony on Saturday night she'd been facing them both. That must be why he unsettled her so much. She could face down her countrymen and flash back at them the image of the arrogant gypsy. But Ricardo Swan was outside her experience. Anglo when she expected him to be Latin. Latin when she thought he was Anglo.

'If you accepted the handbag from me, what costume would you wear with it?'

'One you would not recognise me in.' When the curiosity came alive in his face she realised she'd given the wrong answer.

'I'll always recognise you, Maria. Do you want more to eat?'

'No.' She was moving at his side as if they were friends. She knew that she should try to get away, but running would reveal the kind of panic she had learned not to let anyone see in her. 'I can't eat any more now,' she said absently. 'I'm singing in three hours.'

'You starve yourself before a performance?'

'You can't sing on a full stomach. I'll eat afterwards.'

'Dine with me after the performance tonight.'

'*Gracias, pero no*. I've accepted another invitation.'

'With whom? A lover?'

She shrugged. Fear or nausea welled up in her throat.

'Who is your lover, Maria?'

'Do you expect me to answer you?'

'Come.' His touch on her arm was firm. 'If you won't have dinner with me, come to the children's rides now.'

Surely she could get away if she really tried? People everywhere and all she had to do was go one block away from the roped-off street and find a taxi. A taxi with a very *macho*-looking driver who would not allow the man beside her to follow his fare into the car. Not when she said, '*No! No te quiero*!'

No! I don't want you!

In her mind she'd spoken the familiar pronoun. The intimate *ti*. She didn't want to think of him that way. Better if he remained *usted*—a stranger. His hand was light on her arm, a guiding touch as they went through between the pillars that led to the big courtyard where the travelling circus had erected rides.

'Which do you like?' He gestured and she saw his arm, muscular below the short white sleeve of his shirt.

'The ferris wheel,' she said. Running seemed silly when there were children all around them. He wasn't the monster she'd fantasised on Saturday night. He was a strange mix of worlds but although he wanted her he

had touched her only with the accepted courtesy of a
man escorting a woman he respected.

She would give him an hour. After that she would
never see him again...unless an accident of lighting
brought him to her across the barrier between performer
and audience.

She sat down against one corner of the seat on the
ferris wheel. When he joined her he smiled and she let
herself smile back. She knew that he wanted the passion
of La Gitana. She could have told him there was no
passion in her, but she knew he would not believe her.
He'd seen her dance and he thought he knew what she
was. He was not the first to think that the illusion she
played was reality. He'd penetrated further than the
others. His arms around her on the dance-floor. That
conversation on the balcony. He'd offered her an insult
there, a Spaniard's court paid to a woman he desired.
Not courtship for marriage but an *alianza*. A bargain.
He would give her gifts and she would return passion.

No matter. Two more days and she would be gone
from Mérida.

She settled into the corner as the wheel shifted to let
the next couple board. 'Tell me how you got a name like
Ricardo and Swan?' she asked. 'Latin and gringo?'

'Quite simply,' he said, but she thought that there
wasn't much about him that was simple. 'My father was
a Canadian. He met my mother when he was visiting
Quito. He married her and brought her to Montreal to
live.'

'*Parlez-vous français*?' She didn't know where her
laugh came from. It was breathy and excited, a sound
she might make on stage. 'Where do you belong?' she
asked hurriedly, running from her own confusion.
'Ecuador? French Canada? Digging up Mayan ruins in

Mexico? And you're attached to a university in the States, aren't you?'

'UCLA.'

The air went out of her. Los Angeles. Why must she associate him with that place, with memories that belonged to another life? 'Are you going back?' she asked.

'Perhaps,' he agreed idly.

The wheel started into motion and they rose above the surroundings. She looked down on the colourful street outside the wall. Artisans and their wares, Mexicans and tourists milling through the colours and the noise.

'Maria, where do you go when you leave Mérida?'

She didn't answer.

'I'll find out,' he said softly.

'No one follows me when I leave,' she said flatly, but she shivered as if he had found all her secrets.

'I will.' He said it like a promise. A threat.

She saw the city over his shoulder, the children down below. She was safe enough here. For a short while she could pretend that they were playing the game she acted on stage. Here above the city, soft talk and gazes linking with breathless excitement. An afternoon's fantasy.

'I think you like the Mayan people because they are gone,' she teased. 'They cannot talk back to you.'

A muscle at the side of his mouth twitched in the beginning of a smile. 'And why do I like you?'

'Perhaps you don't like me at all.' She studied the deep lines of his face, the narrowed eyes that were so heavily shadowed. 'Certainly you don't approve of me.'

He shook his head although he did not deny her words. 'What else do you think you know of me?'

'That you want to be the one in control.' She curled her fingers into a fist. 'That you're a mystery.'

He laughed then. 'You're the mystery, gypsy girl.'

She shrugged with deliberate laziness. 'I'm no mystery. I sing for my living. I dress up as a gypsy. But you study the past while everything about you says that you are wealthy and powerful in today's world.'

'My wealth interests you?' He asked the question so quietly that she might have missed the tension in him if she had not been looking.

'Yes,' she agreed. 'I'm curious.' Let him think that she coveted the gifts he could give her. In a day or two it wouldn't matter.

Later, dressing for the performance, she had trouble believing the afternoon had actually happened. She wasn't sure how he'd done it, but he'd had her laughing as they rode on the ferris wheel. He'd pointed out the people below and told her about carnival in Rio. She'd teased him that he'd been everywhere and probably couldn't tell the places apart any more.

'True enough,' he'd agreed with a laugh, but she'd heard the weariness behind the laughter. Then he'd told her about the Galapagos in his mother's country of Ecuador and she'd told him how the beach spread out white and forever for swimming in front of her family's home.

'Where?' he'd asked.

'I'm not telling.' She'd laughed as she denied his curiosity. 'I'll be like the gypsy,' she informed him with a wave of her hand. '*Mañana* I'll be gone.'

'I'll find you.'

'*Nunca*! Never!'

He reached across the distance between them and caught her hair with his fingers.

'Don't!' she gasped. 'I——'

He did something to the string that held her hair back, and her waves went tumbling down all around her shoulders. 'That's better,' he said, his voice husky.

She turned away from him and stared down at the people foreshortened below her. She gathered her hair in both hands and tried to subdue it. He'd taken the string that held it and the curls twisted free again as she tried to contain them. In the end she shook it loose and began to talk as if words could hide her confusion.

'See the hillside where the houses go up forever? I went walking there last week. There's a market there that feels just like the booths at carnival. But it's there every day. Old men with magic hands making carvings right there. Women with the weaving. Children...'

Children—they were talking about children. He told her that he had two nieces and a nephew in Ecuador. She heard the warmth in his voice and thought that his young *sobrinos* probably worshipped their uncle.

'Do you see them often?'

'Once or twice a year,' he replied.

He hadn't asked again where she was going when she left Mérida. It was a game and he had to know that she would win, that she would give her last performance and disappear. He wanted La Gitana but that woman was as insubstantial as mist. When she danced, the gypsy caught her soul a little. She thought that Ricardo was caught in the same trap, and up there above the city she almost wished she could play the game he wanted.

Lovers.

Then the wheel stopped and she got off quickly, looking back at him warily.

'I have to go,' she said breathlessly, and she ran away through the crowd before he could follow.

Fantasy had always been the safest place for her.

\* \* \*

'You've lost weight,' said her mother as she adjusted the waistband of the red satin dress. 'You don't eat enough.'

Maria closed her eyes and stood very still as her mother bent over the dress. 'We'll be home soon,' she reassured her mother. 'Then you know I'll eat.' Would he be in the audience tonight? Would she be able to forget his eyes when the music came?

On stage, she would be safe. If she thought of Ricardo at all, she would picture those moments on the ferris wheel when it had seemed perfectly safe to laugh and tease him.

'I'll find you...'

'Just two more performances,' said her mother. 'You are sure you will be OK if I leave tomorrow before your performance?'

'Of course.' Maria knew that her mother liked to return home ahead of them. To be sure everything was ready, to bring in food and ready their rooms although she knew that Miguel's wife Ana would have done everything that was necessary. 'Give Nita a kiss for me,' she instructed her mother.

The older woman concentrated on adjusting the fall of Maria's hair. 'Your brother Miguel has a baby with his Ana. Soon, you'll see, Emilio too. There will be a girl and they will marry.'

Maria grinned. 'Emilio loves all the girls. Right now he's pursuing Señor Descanso's niece, and she's not even blonde.'

'*He* sent flowers to you again.' Her mother's hands were impatient on her hair. 'Miguel has made enquiries discreetly. He is Dr Ricardo Swan Alantes. A wealthy man.'

Diamonds? she'd asked. If you're worth it, he'd said.

'Miguel told me that you danced with him at Señor Descanso's mansion on Saturday?'

Maria looked down at her mother's matronly shape. At her frown. 'Yes,' she agreed. 'I danced with him. Once. I also danced with Señor Descanso. He invited me to dinner with his wife in Mexico City.'

'Dr Swan has sent roses, and invitations.'

Maria moved away to stand in front of the mirror. Her reflection showed a passionate-looking woman dressed in red. Red lips and brunette hair with rich red highlights. Red like the roses on the table near the window.

'Send the flowers to the orphanage,' she said. In the mirror Maria saw her mother shake her head with disapproval.

'There's an envelope. Perhaps an invitation.'

Maria sighed. '*Mamá mía*, I know you want me to find a nice man and get married. But—not everyone needs a husband.'

'My Maria does.' Her mother was at the flowers, a beautifully rounded mature woman who had loved her father passionately and happily through all their lives. Maria didn't know what to say. She'd never known how to answer her mother on this issue. Miguel was the only one who understood.

'You can't live all your life on the stage,' her mother muttered.

'Ricardo Swan wants what they all want.' She turned to face her mother. She was ready to go on stage, her head high with Spanish arrogance that was more powerful than the sensuality Ricardo wanted to possess. 'It's time, isn't it? Miguel will have the car downstairs.'

'Read the note,' insisted her mother.

'After, perhaps.'

The maid was at the door as they went out. Maria stopped to talk to her. 'Would you arrange for these roses to be sent to the orphanage, *por favor*?'

Behind her, Maria heard her *mamá* protest.

As she sang that night in the open air, she sang to the crowd and the crowd had no name. She could not see Ricardo and she told herself that she was safe with the music around her and the crowd in front of her.

They fell quiet when she sang the Lisbon love song. It was a song for breathless listening. She could see the audience as a mass of shapes beyond the lights. She ended the song with her eyes fixed on the shape of a man standing to one side, higher up than the others. A tall man, head and shoulders plain in the crowd.

She didn't want it to be him.

In the taxi going back to the hotel she rode in front where there was room for the heavy folds of her dress to spread out around her. Her brothers and her mother rode in the back.

Two blocks from the hotel Miguel spoke.

'Dr Swan has made us an invitation for tomorrow night. A small party at Los Arcos for dinner after your last performance.'

'No!'

She twisted around and they were all staring at her from the back seat, Emilio shaking his head and her mother and Miguel frowning.

'Maria,' warned Miguel, 'you must be reasonable.'

She twisted to face forward. The taxi driver was watching her with that same look in his eyes. Did all the men in the world want only one thing? Why must they look at *her* with demanding desire in their eyes?

'I don't like him,' she muttered.

Emilio leaned forward and put an impatient hand on her shoulder. 'Señor Descanso and his niece have been invited. Don't spoil the party, Maria. He's been sending you roses all week.'

She closed her eyes. 'If you want to see the niece, do it on your own. Count me out of it.' Gifts. Roses. The beautiful handbag he had bought for her. On the dance-floor, his touch on her and she'd asked if he would give her diamonds. 'Only if you're very good...'

Good at loving. At passion.

'No!' she said again, and the taxi driver jerked the steering-wheel. 'I won't go.'

In the back seat, no one said a word.

At the hotel, Miguel followed her up to her room. Maria went to the window, pulling the ivory combs out of her hair, discarding them on the table. Her brother was behind her.

'Pour yourself a drink,' she said.

She heard the sounds as he poured himself a glass of tequila. The flowers were gone from the little table. There were other flowers from other admirers, but the red roses were gone. The small envelope with her name on it was on the table where the roses had been. She didn't have to read what was inside to know it would be an invitation. Dinner tomorrow night. Her family was going to pressure her into saying yes.

'Mamá is naïve,' she said. She didn't look at Miguel. She could hear him pacing behind her and knew that he would tell her his mind soon enough. She could see the shapes of tall palms blowing gently in the breeze across the street. 'Mamá thinks Dr Swan is courting me. She sees wedding bells.'

Miguel stopped pacing. 'He's invited us to dine with a very important group of people. It would be rude to refuse.'

She turned angrily away from the window. He had the glass in his hand, his reasonable look on his face. 'I'm tired. You go if you like, but I won't go!'

He shook his head sharply. 'It's hardly professional to refuse a dinner party in your honour when it's given by a wealthy and prestigious man who has invited the mayor among others.'

'You know what he wants.' She looked away from him. 'And I don't—I don't like him.'

Miguel sighed. '*Chica*, be reasonable. I'll be there, and Emilio. And if he asks you to have dinner alone with him on some future occasion——' Miguel smiled. 'You're good at saying no. Why should this invitation be a problem? At Los Arcos with other guests. A gesture of admiration he makes for a great performer.'

Ricardo had trapped her again, just as he had trapped her into dancing with him last Saturday. No force and yet she had no choice. And today on the streets—why had she let him keep her at his side all through the afternoon? Eating hot dogs with him and strolling along the displays of crafts. Going on the ferris wheel where she'd relaxed because in a couple of hours she would never see him again.

'Will there be dancing?'

'I imagine so.'

Maria swallowed. 'I don't want to dance with him.'

'Emilio said you danced with him last Saturday night at Descanso's.' Miguel stiffened. 'Did he——?'

'No.' She shook her head, knowing Miguel would fly to her defence if he thought anyone was giving her that kind of trouble. 'He danced with me, and we talked. I just don't . . . I don't like him.'

Miguel obviously thought she was making an issue out of nothing but he shrugged his agreement. '*Está bien*. We'll say you've sprained your ankle in the performance. You won't dance at all.'

Conversation over dinner. She could handle that if she avoided his eyes. If Ricardo placed her at his side, she would turn to the man on her other side. With luck it would be Señor Descanso or Miguel.

And if Dr Swan tried to pressure her into accepting a more intimate invitation, she would tell her brother. Miguel was good at being intimidating to her admirers. He didn't pressure her to take an interest in men the way her mother did. He understood that she did not want any men in her life but her brothers.

No lovers.

# CHAPTER FOUR

THE note was delivered with Maria's breakfast. She saw the white envelope the instant the waiter handed her the tray. It was leaning against a tall, thin glass vase that held a single red rose.

She got back into bed and put the tray across her knees. The coffee the waiter had brought was tepid and too strong. She drank it slowly as she stared at the envelope. Her name, written in *his* hand. She had seen that thick strong handwriting too often this week. He knew her name, knew her last name. How had he known? She was La Gitana to the public. Her legal name wasn't exactly a secret, but neither was it a matter of common knowledge.

How had he known she would be at that party Saturday night?

He knew which hotel she stayed in. Again, not a secret, but...

'I'll find you...'

She put her cup down with a thud. The location of the Concerta family home was something no one knew. Her father had insisted on the secrecy and they'd all kept it up even after his death. Miguel and Ana wanted their children to grow up without the worry of photographers and news people. Maria wanted a private life completely separate from her public, and while her mother didn't seem to understand that, Miguel did. And Miguel managed the family's finances and her publicity.

Ricardo *couldn't* find her home. Tomorrow morning she would fly away from Mérida. Tomorrow the roses would stop. He would not know where to send them. In a few days or a few weeks he would tire of his curiosity.

'I never could resist a mystery...'

He was a man who had spent years of work to satisfy his curiosity about history, although he had no need to work. She pushed the tray aside. How much effort would he expend to find her?

The envelope was sealed. She opened it.

I can offer Mayan carvings and a breath of yesterday. Meet me at ten at Hot Dogs Exquisitos. A suitable costume for this performance would be jeans and tennis shoes—the ponytail if you must. Bring a hat against the sun. I'll be waiting. Ricardo.

Of course she wouldn't go. She would rest here in her room. It had been a long week of performances and she needed a day of rest.

Normally she would have gone down to the carnival again, dressed as a tourist, but yesterday he had recognised her in her tourist costume. She had always been safe dressed like that: no make-up, no costume wardrobe, her long hair trapped in a casual ponytail. Presto! La Gitana was gone. She'd always felt so pleased about that.

How had he recognised La Gitana when the gypsy was only a fantasy on stage? Something in her walk, he had said. 'When you begin to walk—then La Gitana reveals herself...' She shuddered and threw the covers aside.

Tonight, at dinner, he would ask what she'd done today. A formal question, but his eyes would tell her that he intended to possess her. Diamonds...if she was very good!

She dared not go out of her room until tonight's performance. He had found her at that party and again on the streets yesterday. He'd manipulated her into attending this dinner tonight and she was trapped in it, caught in a lie about a sore ankle to avoid his arms around her.

She dressed quickly, slipping into the jeans and a fresh cotton shirt. So hot already! Early March and it should have been cooler in the mornings. She'd always heard that Mérida had a reputation for being deadly hot even in winter and it was true. If only she were home! If only she could escape the confinement of this room by running down to the beach and into the water! The water had been cool when she left home a month ago. She liked that, liked the breathless feel of cool water under the sun's heat and the knowledge that she was alone. It would be warmer now, and she would have to stick to the beach directly outside their *casa* to avoid the tourists who had beach houses nearer to San Jose del Cabo. But she would be safe there. And free.

All day here in this room.

She was pacing already. Trembling with the trap of this room and all the long hours of the day ahead. Her mother was gone, driven to the airport by Miguel who had said he would attend to the business meeting with Señor Descanso before he returned to the hotel. Emilio had said, good, he'd sleep in. That left Maria with nothing to do, no practice session to use up the hours.

The performance. Then dinner. Ricardo would be watching her all through the dinner. He would arrange the seating, of course. If he wanted her at his side——

She spun to the window abruptly. Trapped in this room all day! She could go mad! Mamá was right, Maria ate too little when she was on tour, lived on her nerves and could not relax until it was over and she was home again.

Ridiculous that she should be imprisoned here all day because of *him*! Surely Mérida was big enough that she needn't be a prisoner all day?

What if she went with him to look at the Mayan ruins? What would happen? He'd mentioned a car he kept down here. He would be driving. An hour in a car with both his hands on the wheel. It would be as safe as the ferris wheel had been. At the ruins there would be others, the students he had mentioned and perhaps the blonde woman who had been with him at the club and the party. The married woman whom gossip said Ricardo had wanted for himself.

He had no right to imprison her with the threat of his pursuit. She would not let him trap her! She would go out on to the streets—just not *that* street.

She dressed quickly and ran down the carpeted stairs that led to the ground level of her hotel. Outside, the walls of the old colonial buildings of Mérida seemed to reflect back the heat of the morning sun and the crowds. It was Mardi Gras, the last day of carnival. The excitement was in the streets. Brilliant costumes in the crowd. The colourful display for the Mardi Gras parade. Later there would be folk dancing and athletic events.

If he had suggested that she come out to share in the street dancing, she would not even have felt temptation. That was what made him dangerous. People flocked to Mérida for its Mardi Gras celebration, but Ricardo Swan suggested she spend the day away from the city. A day of quiet for the woman who would perform in front of the crowds tonight.

She wasn't interested in his Mayans. History was past and gone. If he had suggested a day on the beach he might have tempted her to take a chance. But he hadn't mentioned the beaches thirty kilometres away and he didn't tempt her. She'd dreamed of him once last week and it had frightened her that he got into her sleep. But not last night. Last night was a reassuring blank. No dreams.

She ran quickly through the streets. She was a tourist again. She didn't meet the eyes of the young men on the prowl through the crowds. She wasn't worried about them. She knew how to turn her own countrymen's advances off with a sharp '*No*!' and a refusal to exchange gazes. That was where she'd made her mistake with Ricardo. She had let herself get caught in the trap of his gaze when she was on stage at La Casa del Viento. Then she had looked up and stared into his eyes the night he danced with her and let her know in no uncertain terms that he intended to be her lover.

He had no real power if she simply refused to meet his eyes. He wanted her as a lover, but she was not the woman he had dreamed of when he watched her on stage. The sensuous and mysterious creature who danced and sang of love and anger was a creature of make-believe. She was Maria Concerta, a good girl. And she had Miguel near her always to ensure that no man overstepped the bounds she set.

Dinner in public with others . . . yes.

Together alone . . . loving and touching—no!

He was near the hot dog stand, wearing lightweight trousers and a pale brown cotton guayabera that made him look very Latin. He was talking to an old man leaning on a cane. As she came around the end of the last stall before the corner the old man laughed and she saw Ricardo grin in response. Then he saw her. He said something to the man at his side and came quickly towards Maria.

She stopped, suddenly dizzy with the sensation that she was being drawn towards him too fast... that when she reached him his arms would be around her and she'd be drowning in the heavy heartbeat that had been on her when she woke in the night.

She hadn't dreamed. She *hadn't*. Not of him.

'Maria,' he said. Nothing more than that. Her name on his lips and she felt her throat so dry that she had to swallow before she could speak. He was looking at her with a smile of victory as if he had known she would come.

'Ricardo, I—I'm not coming out with you today.'

She saw his lips curve in a smile that brought a tremble to her hands. 'Jeans,' he said. 'And the ponytail. You forgot the hat.'

'I'm not going with——'

'Yes, you are.' His hand fastened on her upper arm. 'Play games if you must, but don't imagine it deceives me.' The muscle that jumped in his jaw was her only signal that she should discount the smile on his lips.

'I want to watch the parade,' she insisted.

'If you were interested in the parade you'd be in it.'

'They wanted me to, but Miguel refused.' She pressed her lips together, then said, 'I don't want this.'

'Another move in the dance of seduction?' His voice was dangerously soft. 'Make your moves... retreat and advance. Look at me through those black eyelashes and tell me you don't want me. But remember—I understand your game.'

'No! It's not—not a game.'

'Of course it is. I saw you dance. I see you now. There's no difference. Your arrogant dance of seduction, tempting a man...then spinning back with your eyes wide and naïve.' He shrugged and the predator was gone from his eyes. '*Está bien*, La Gitana. I'll play your game.'

He didn't believe her. He read some imaginary signal in her eyes and it was a lie. What was it in her eyes? In her walk? Signals she didn't want to give him... but she couldn't find the key to stop them.

His hand possessed her arm. 'My car's a block away,' he murmured. He shielded her from the crowd as he moved.

'Where——?'

He stopped at a stall spilling over with hats. He reached for a straw hat with a red sash streaming off one side. She felt it settle over her hair. Ricardo studied her through narrowed eyes.

'A good costume,' he decided.

She reached up to remove the hat. 'I'm not going.'

His hand intercepted hers and he tangled his fingers in hers. 'It'll be a hot day. The streets of Mérida are almost unbearable and you'll be performing tonight in that heavy gown.'

'I—I don't...want...' She brushed her free hand across her cheek, conscious of heat prickling between her shoulder-blades as if he had hypnotised her.

'There's a public beach at Progreso a few miles past the archaeological site.'

White sand and she could take her shoes off and walk in the shallow water.

'I'll show you the archaeological site at Dzibilchaltún and then the beach at Progreso. We'll have a truce this one morning.'

'Your excavation? I thought it was to the south?'

'Yes, it is, but I'm not taking you there. We'll go north where there's a beach.'

She bit her lip. 'I don't want to be involved with you,' she said soberly. 'If I go with you, all that will happen is that you'll show me the Mayan carvings and—and then I'll go away. I'll never see you again.'

'You're having dinner with me tonight,' he reminded her. 'Your brother sent word that your family has accepted my invitation . . . with the exception of your mother.'

'She's gone ahead of us, gone home.'

'To——?'

She shook her head. 'I won't tell you where I live. I won't dance with you tonight either.' She lifted her head slightly. 'I plan to have a sore ankle after the performance.'

'Then as your host I must stay at your side to keep you from being bored by your enforced inactivity.'

'The beach first?' she asked breathlessly. 'Could we go to the beach before the archaeological site.'

'Do you think I mean to lecture you on the past?' The thought seemed to amuse him greatly. 'You're like a child. First play.'

'I'll work tonight,' she said.

He frowned at her. 'I doubt you think of it as work. When you're on that stage——'

'Don't talk about La Gitana!' she said sharply. 'If you must, then talk about the Maya—although I don't know that I'm interested in your old carvings. You might well lecture me. Sometimes you lecture university students in the States, don't you?'

Laughter gave his voice a warm timbre. 'I can survive months at a time without giving way to the urge to lecture. Come on, then. After all it is Mardi Gras—Fat

Tuesday as the English would translate it. We'll play. In Peru the *campesinos* call carnival-time *pukllay taki*.'

'What does that mean?'

'It translates as "let's play".'

'Do you know Peru well?' Asking questions, telling herself she would say no when he actually started trying to walk her to his vehicle.

'Short visits, but a friend of mine is married to a Peruvian landowner.'

'Oh. The blonde woman at the party?'

'Cathy. Yes.' He made a gesture in what must be the direction of north. To the beach.

'She is very beautiful,' Maria said.

'Yes,' agreed Ricardo.

Perhaps he *was* the American woman's lover. Men didn't always keep the marriage vow, although the blonde woman had looked radiantly in love and also pregnant. A woman glorying in the excitement of bearing her husband's child.

Maria shook off an unexpected wave of envy. She had no need of her own children, not when having a baby meant having a man first. She preferred to keep the men on the other side of the barrier between performer and audience.

'I'll be gone tomorrow,' she reminded him.

'We'll have today first,' he said easily, as if her leaving meant nothing.

What danger was there on a sunny day in March on a public beach? He was a man of stature. Such a man would not prey on a woman who had men in her family to protect her good name. He might try to seduce her with words, but all she had to do was refuse his offers. He would surely never force her.

He was only another man with bold eyes. Another man who thought the dancer was the reality, who thought *she* was trying to seduce him. It was years since she'd been close enough to a man to hear that accusation. Not since she was seventeen. Nine years ago and a world away.

Not since Los Angeles. Not since Wallace.

Ricardo's car was a jeep with a quiet engine and open windows that let the wind through. He frowned when Maria took off her hat.

'The top will shade me from the sun,' she said defensively. Immediately, she felt angry at her words. Excusing herself as if he had authority over her. 'I never sunburn,' she added. 'Not like your blonde friend.'

He studied her expression for so long she had trouble sitting still. 'I wonder what you're really thinking?' he said finally.

'Go on wondering,' she suggested. 'I don't share.'

He let his gaze slide down the creamy length of her throat to the swelling of her breasts under the cotton blouse. 'Neither do I,' he said slowly. 'In particular, I don't share my women.'

'Congratulations.' Her voice was caustic. 'Are we going to the beach or not? The seats in this jeep are too hot for sitting around.'

Something flashed over his face. Anger, and for a moment she thought he would reach out and possess her face with his hand... bring her mouth to his and force a hard kiss on her.

'I've changed my mind,' she whispered. Her breathing made her words jerky. 'I don't want to go to the beach.'

He turned the key.

She reached for the door-handle.

He shoved the gear-shift lever forward and flashed his hand across to grasp her wrist.

'Let me go!' she yelped.

'I'll play this game only so far, Maria.'

'You're hurting my wrist!' The pain was in her chest, not her wrist, but she pulled against his grip. 'Let go of me!'

'Let go of the door first.'

She shook her head. She tightened her free hand's grip on the door-handle. Her other hand was raised, poised above her lap and trapped in his grasp.

'We can drive like this all the way to Progreso,' he said. 'Or you can relax and stop playing games that go nowhere.'

'I don't want to go anywhere.' She gulped and her hand began to tremble from the strain of holding it still, poised above her lap and trapped by his. What insanity had brought her out to meet him today? As if she *wanted* to go into danger.

He must have let go the clutch because they were in motion and her hand was still in his grasp while he controlled the wheel with his free hand. She stared directly ahead. A young Mexican boy moved to one side, then Ricardo stopped the jeep's motion while three middle-aged women moved across in front of them.

'Will you go all the way to Progreso in low gear?' she demanded, pulling against his grip.

'If necessary.'

'I don't want to go with you.'

'You should have thought of that earlier.'

'Yes,' she admitted desperately.

The car was moving faster now, the crowds parting for him. She looked around wildly. Was he like Wallace? Hearing one thing when she said another and in the end—he wasn't going to stop. He drove past a policeman who turned his head to look curiously at their raised hands locked together. The last glimpse Maria had of the policeman was his uniformed arm raised in a gesture of salute.

'Since you're not going to call for help,' said Ricardo, 'and as I've no intention of letting you change your mind about coming with me, why don't you let go of that door?'

She bit her lip. 'You let go of me first.'

'And be responsible for your leaping out of a moving vehicle? Hardly.'

She knew there was no real choice. She could hang on to the door all the way to Progreso and suffer his grip on her wrist like a child being disciplined, or she could give in. She let the handle go.

He released her wrist.

She didn't look at him, although she could see his hand on the gear-shift lever. She could see the edges of him without looking. His hand and a muscled forearm. His thigh under the dark fabric of his trousers.

'You may as well stop sulking,' he suggested mildly. 'I have three sisters and an emotional Latin *mamá*. I can assure you I'm immune to both sulks and displays of temper.'

She felt a muscle in her jaw jerk with tension. 'I don't sulk.'

'It's a good performance, then. It fooled me.'

A traitorous bubble of laughter pressed against her throat. 'I am a performer,' she said, but her voice sounded so stuffy that the laugh followed her words.

He flashed her a look that held a warmth she hadn't seen in him before. 'I promise you, Maria Concerta, I'll uncover your layers until there's no doubt which of the parts you play is the real woman.'

'That may be difficult,' she said stiffly. 'Tomorrow I'll be gone. I won't be leaving a trail for you to follow, nor an invitation.'

Because it was the last and most elaborate day of carnival, the beaches at Progreso were deserted except for a few of the locals. The tourists had gone to find the street celebrations.

'Take your shoes off,' Ricardo suggested when she stepped on to the beach.

Ever since their skirmish back in the outskirts of Mérida, he had seemed relaxed and easy to be with. Now he was watching the shore beyond her as he made the suggestion.

She dropped down on the sand to slip off her shoes, then rolled up the legs of her jeans so that they wouldn't get wet if she waded into the surf. 'My mother wouldn't approve,' she said when she stood up.

He had shed his shoes and socks as well. He held out his hand for her shoes and put them into the jeep that was parked on the edge of the beach. 'You're a foreigner today,' he reminded her. 'A tourist in denim and a ponytail.'

She laughed with pleasure at the thought and ran away from him, down the beach. Halfway to the water she looked back in sudden panic, but he was following slowly and he hadn't taken her flight as an invitation to pursue.

Teasing. Seductive teasing. That was what he thought she was doing. He believed in La Gitana and she wasn't doing much of a job of persuading him otherwise. Sometimes when she looked at him she thought that— well, perhaps she was tempted in the moments when he laughed ... or when he looked at her as if he liked what he saw and expected that at any moment she would do something that would excite him beyond bearing. When he looked at her like that it frightened her ... but sometimes it made her wonder what it would be like ...

What would it be like to be in love? What would it be like if she were the woman he thought? If she could let the dance become a dance of seduction to draw him to her woman's spell? She ran into the water and felt the ocean warm against her ankles. She looked back and his smile made her think of a man who enjoyed watching a woman move.

He'd recognised the way she walked. The way she moved. He had recognised her in the crowd yesterday despite her disguise and he thought now that she was playing a game of seduction. That she would be his lover!

She kept reliving the sensation of his hand on her arm. The tingling awareness of his gaze on her body when she was helpless and too much a woman in her dreams on stage. Temptation ... when she had believed she could never be tempted again. What would his lips feel like on hers?

Tonight was the last time she would ever see him. What if she allowed him to kiss her? Perhaps she would let herself dance with him. Just once, and he would find a way to stop their motion away from the others ... on the balcony with moonlight coming down over them ... his hand on her back ... sensations on the naked flesh of her back above the dress ... his kiss ... edges of fantasy from a dream she'd tried to deny having ... lips full and firm ... taking her mouth ... her body ...

She bent down and splashed up water from the sea, felt the wetness against her lips and shuddered at the imagined touch of his mouth both soft and hard against hers. Demanding.

In the real world his kiss would demand more than she could give.

No! Just one kiss and she would slip away and he would be a dream lover. Dream lovers didn't have the power to turn excitement into nightmares. In dreams, as on stage, she could move any way she wished. No one could touch her.

He caught her hand as she walked in the shallows of the sea. There were other people all around. She knew she should pull away, knew the fantasy of one kiss was too dangerous...but his hand held hers and she didn't let herself look down at the place where his brown fingers tangled with her hand. She could feel his maleness in that grip. Hard brown flesh that held strength and a texture that made her picture him working, the play of his muscles through the thin cotton of his shirt. In Mexico a man didn't take off his shirt in public, but Ricardo lived in the States where a man might be seen naked from the waist up. Ricardo naked above the belt that held his jeans...Ricardo...she might see him like that in his own yard when it was summer. He would strip off the shirt and throw it to one side. Reach down for some foggy tool she couldn't quite picture and lift it in a swing of musculature.

'Do you have a house in the States?' Her question was breathless. 'A yard?'

'Yes, but I'm not there that much.'

'Where——?' She had to stop this! His hand holding hers and his eyes warm and curious so that she had a frightening feeling that he was about to...

'Would you like to visit me there?' He asked the question so quietly that she didn't feel the meaning of the words for several seconds.

She pulled and his grip tightened, then suddenly she was free and staring at him. He was staring back as if she were on the stage. 'No,' she said. 'Stop that!'

'Stop what?'

'This game! This—this——! *Dios*! I am not a game you play!'

'Aren't you?' His mouth curved and she could not tell if it was amusement or irritation. 'You're the one playing a game. We both know where it will end.'

She tilted her head higher and as she moved she saw herself as if she were the one watching. Her head high and angry. Her eyes narrowed. She'd seen her costumed image on a replay of a live television appearance and she recognised the tension of the way she held her body now. As if she were playing a part.

That was what he saw.

'I want to leave now,' she said stiffly.

# CHAPTER FIVE

THE crowd was high on Mardi Gras spirit. With every movement Maria made she could hear the people of Mérida echoing back their pleasure. Miguel had done something to the lighting that he said would make her dress glisten as if in moonlight. As she moved in the spell of the music from Emilio's guitar she could feel both her own rhythm and the echo of the music from the audience.

She had performed a few times up in the States, once on television and one tour through California and Nevada. American audiences were never like this, reflecting the excitement of the music back to her. Perhaps because passions ran closer to the surface south of the border between the States and Mexico.

Whatever the reason, Maria could feel the pleasure of the audience and she became even more the gypsy. She ceased to be Maria, a woman mostly of Spanish descent with a little American thrown in from her grandmother. She became an Andalusian singing and dancing the pride and the anger of her ancestors. She was controlled passion boiling into music, a woman aware of her sex and her ancestry and flaunting both with pride.

Ricardo was there in the images that flowed across her mind with the song. Ricardo as she remembered him from earlier in the day. He had stopped the jeep on the way back to Mérida at the archaeological site of Dzibilchaltún. They had walked together into the Temple of the Seven Dolls. They had not touched in any way in the temple, but Maria had been aware of his every motion as his voice spoke to her. She had asked questions, aware that she wanted to hear the sound of his voice more than the answers about the Mayan past. But his words had painted pictures on her mind and although he had seemed purely gringo in those moments staring at the exhibits, her imagination had drawn confusing sensations and impossible desires.

She had suppressed both then, but now they came to the surface. When the song ended and the dance began her body moved with its own will to the music. In fantasy she went back to the Cenote Xlacah—the pool of deep water at the archaeological site. Ricardo had told her that the greenish-blue pool had given up over thirty thousand Mayan artefacts to divers. He'd spoken of the mystery and she'd felt other words lying under the surface. She'd moved out from his reach when she realised there was no one near them and she could *feel* that he had the urge to catch her in his arms and show her what loving would be for them.

'The Mayan priests used to sing,' he'd told her as they stared at each other beside the deep pool.

'What did they sing?'

'Come, children...hurry, children...worship the sun.'

In the dance she was free to answer the look she'd seen in his eyes. In the song she could answer him without fear. And as she made her final bow to the roar of the Mardi Gras crowd she felt the reckless wildness of La Gitana as if the performance were still on her.

Afterwards, in the taxi with Miguel and Emilio, Miguel turned as always to practical details. 'You'll want to change before we go to dine, Maria?'

'No,' she answered, staring ahead through the windscreen of the taxi. 'La Gitana was invited to dinner. This is the gypsy—this costume.'

'It's too hot.' She could hear the frown in his voice.

She shrugged and let him have his way. In her room she put music on and struggled out of the red gown. Usually her mother helped her with this. The gown was designed with a long zip up the back that was hard to reach. She threw it on the bed when she was free of it. It lay there in a swirl of magic that blended with the music on the radio. She twisted her hair up out of the way and went into the shower. She sang softly as she washed away the heat of the night.

A command performance to dine. There would be music made by others. Dancing, and she had told Ricardo that she planned to have a sore ankle. She selected red from the wardrobe where her clothes hung. A long red silk dress that bared her shoulders and clung to her body with a subtle caress that did not show until she moved under the lights. The dress was cut high in the bodice and low in the back. The skirt fell straight to the floor with only enough flare to make it possible to dance. It was not a costume for flamenco, but she had worn it for the television performance in the States and she used it now sometimes as a costume for social appearances in the evening. It was a public dress designed to remind people of the image she projected on stage.

She could feel her hair drifting across the naked flesh of her back as she moved to the door. It reminded her of Ricardo's fingers touching the bare skin of her back when they'd danced.

Miguel frowned when he saw the gown. 'Don't forget to limp,' he warned.

Emilio was grinning. 'I always liked that dress. Why would you limp?'

'She doesn't want to dance,' said Miguel repressively.

Maria stared forward through the windscreen as they drove to Los Arcos. In the back seat her brothers were discussing the performance. When they tossed questions or comments at her she did not reply. They didn't insist on her answers. She was often quiet after a performance, still caught in the spell of the role she played.

Tomorrow she would leave this place, but tonight she was La Gitana.

It was almost midnight when she entered Los Arcos with her brothers. She saw Ricardo as soon as she came into the room. He stood when he saw her. She gripped Miguel's arm more tightly and let her eyes half close. This was her last performance in Mérida. Tomorrow was Ash Wednesday. Carnival would be over and she would leave Mérida and Ricardo behind.

She felt as if she were gliding across the room. With her hands resting on her brothers' arms, she moved in the wake of the *maître d'*. People stopped talking as she passed. The wave of silence that swept through the restaurant in her wake heightened her sensation of being on stage.

'Remember the ankle,' murmured Miguel.

'Yes,' she agreed without looking at him.

Ricardo moved to hold her chair for her. She stared straight ahead as he seated her and when his fingers brushed the flesh of her back below the fall of her hair she hardly trembled at all.

She was seated at Ricardo's right hand. Miguel was seated across from her and one seat further down the table. Emilio sat beside her with Señor Descanso's niece on his right. The other members of the party were Señor

Descanso himself, the mayor and his wife, the blonde archaeologist Dr Catherine Jenan and her dark handsome husband Juan Corsica who had arrived from Paris that afternoon.

'We were married in Mérida last August,' Maria overhead the blonde woman explaining to the mayor. 'It seems only right that we celebrate Mardi Gras here.'

She saw Ricardo frown as Cathy's voice drifted along the length of the table. Was it true that he had wanted the blonde woman himself? Were they lovers even now?

'What are you thinking?' his voice demanded quietly.

She let her eyelashes drop to cover anything he might see there. He had arranged the seating deliberately. Emilio at her side and he was focused on the pretty niece. The mayor's wife at Ricardo's other side, and she seemed fascinated by Miguel who was beside her. That left Ricardo and Maria isolated from the others. When she let herself look up at him she felt his awareness as a tingle of electricity crawling down her back.

'What are you thinking?' he asked again.

'That carnival ends tonight. Nothing else.'

'Should I believe that?'

'Believe what you want,' she said quietly. 'That's the nature of a performance. The audience reads what they choose into the artist's message.'

'Is this a performance?' His gaze dropped to take in the red silk covering the swelling of her breasts. Then he was staring at the stage rings still on the fingers of her hand as it lay curved around her glass.

She smiled the gypsy's smile. 'Of course it's a performance,' she said. 'You must tell me if it's a good performance.'

He lifted his glass towards hers in a gesture of mocking homage. 'La Gitana,' he murmured. 'You hardly need an answer to that.'

She lifted her glass to her lips and sipped as he did. He watched her taking the red wine with her lips and she felt as if he had touched his mouth to hers and it was him she tasted.

'Dance with me,' he demanded in a low voice.

'You've forgotten my ankle.' She wasn't certain if he could hear her and it hardly seemed to matter.

'I've forgotten nothing.' He pushed his chair back and held his hand out.

Her arm moved . . . hand came to rest on his. She put her drink down and rose slowly as if it were slow music pacing her in a choreography of seduction. A long breath later she was standing. He placed her hand on his arm and turned towards the dance-floor.

A long moment of stillness when his arms reached out to accept her body in the embrace of the dance.

'The dance begins,' he said softly. 'Are you ready, Maria?'

They were on stage, she realised. She and Ricardo and people all around. His hand held out towards her. 'If they take a long breath before the applause begins, it's a good performance,' she said.

'I assure you, they will.'

It was the gypsy who went into his arms. She was on stage and wrapped in the safety of her performance. This was the dance and she could let him guide her . . . could let her eyes hold his in the music. He moved with the restrained grace of a Spaniard, the passion running free in his eyes as they held hers, echoed in his touch so that she could feel his desire even while he restrained his movements to the ritual of the dance.

His hand on her back. Not caressing but touching, fingers spread out so that she felt each place of contact and the message of the seduction that would come later. A dream seduction that had no warning twinge of reality. When the music stopped his hand slid away from her back and left a shudder of sensation in its wake. He caught her hand in his and his eyes widened as if he could feel the tremor that flashed through her. She dropped her eyes quickly and moved in the ritual of a curtsy towards him.

'*Gracias, señorita.*'

'*De nada,*' she murmured.

Miguel intercepted them on their way back to the table. He bowed to them with anger in his eyes as his gaze met his sister's.

'Dance, Maria,' he said. It was an order.

Maria felt Ricardo's hand again at her back as he gave her up into her brother's arms. Then Miguel was moving away with her and she could not look back but she thought Ricardo was not watching, that he had turned away to the table and his other guests.

'Your ankle is better?' demanded Miguel angrily.

She shrugged as she followed his lead in the dance.

'What game are you playing, *chica*? You know what he wants?'

She looked away from her brother's accusing face. A woman sitting at one of the tables waved and Maria smiled back. She didn't answer Miguel.

'I told you to have a sore ankle. You said you didn't want to dance with him.'

'It doesn't matter,' she said tonelessly. 'Tomorrow I leave. As you said, what harm to talk at dinner and dance once or twice?'

Miguel's jaw was thrust out. 'He wants you.'

She gave a small shrug. 'As you pointed out, he isn't the first.'

Miguel turned her to avoid a young man dancing energetically with his *novia*. 'I didn't expect you to be teasing him, looking at him in such a way that he could hardly miss the invitation.'

'I wasn't——' She shook her head, but the heavy beat of her heart frightened her.

Miguel frowned down at her, his eyes suddenly probing. 'Is this man different, Maria? Do you feel something for him?'

'No! No!' She bit her lip and felt her brother's arms catch her as she stumbled.

'I'll talk to him.'

'No!' Her heart was pounding in earnest now. 'No, Miguel. Just—tomorrow we leave. It doesn't matter. I——'

'He might follow.'

She shook her head. 'How can he? He doesn't know where we live.'

'You might tell him if he asks. I saw you dancing with him. Perhaps you want him to follow.'

She said, 'No!' but Miguel didn't seem to hear.

'If you care about this man...' Miguel's face was harsh and lined suddenly. 'Maria, if that is how it is, I'll talk to him.'

If he talked to Ricardo he would make it clear that Maria Concerta would only be pursued by a man with honourable intentions.

'Miguel,' she said sharply, 'I don't want a husband. I don't want any man.'

For the first time, he looked as if he doubted her.

The food arrived as Miguel delivered her back to her seat. She'd been a fool, she realised. She had danced with him as if it were a performance, as if it were safe to lock eyes boldly and make promises without words. Ricardo was a man who wanted her in his bed, who had hinted at diamonds if she were *very good*.

Her face flamed and his real voice demanded, 'What are you thinking that makes you look like that?'

'Nothing.'

He filled her glass again and he drank when she did. 'We'll dance again when the band resumes playing,' he promised.

'I don't want to dance,' she said, but his eyes told her he did not believe her.

He was dressed formally tonight, but she could still see the less formal Ricardo of this afternoon. They might have danced on the rocks at the deep ancient pool of water if she had let the music of history play in her veins. The danger would have been very real in that place. No one but the ghosts to watch.

She sipped her wine and felt the pulse in her throat.

'Will you be leaving now that carnival is over?' asked the mayor's wife from the other side of the table.

'Yes,' said Maria, glad to look away from Ricardo. 'We'll rest at home for a few weeks before our next engagement.'

'You have a place by the ocean, I understand.'

Maria nodded agreement.

'Secret?' asked the woman with faint disdain. 'My daughter read in a magazine that no one knows where your home is located.'

Although the woman was insistent, Maria refused to be drawn about the location of her home. It wasn't the first time she'd had this conversation and she was practised at polite evasion. This time, though, she was aware of Ricardo listening and she remembered his insistence that he would find her.

From across the table, Miguel added his support. 'I have a *niña*,' he explained to the mayor's wife. 'My wife and I want our daughter to live in a normal fashion, without great publicity. And Maria must rest away from the public between performances. Otherwise, she works too hard.'

'What do you do when you rest?' Ricardo asked.

She pushed her plate aside. 'I spend time with my family,' she said. 'Often with my niece. And Emilio and I practise.'

'Tell me more about your niece.'

'She's five years old.' She relaxed slightly as she told him about Nita and the recent escapade when Nita had decided to put on a performance for the village children as a singer accompanied by a young friend on guitar.

'So she isn't quite an ordinary child?' he asked, amused.

'Not quite, I suppose.' She returned his smile. 'We do practise our numbers in the music room at our home and Nita likes to watch.' She smiled. 'She can be a temperamental young charmer, so perhaps she's a bit spoiled, although Ana and Miguel can be quite firm with her. But you understand, we've always had music in my family. My father was a performer and as children we often performed with him.'

'Hmm.' He put down his glass. 'And of course the village where this performance of Nita's occurred has no name.'

'You're right, of course.' She felt her lips curving in a smile. 'A nameless village.'

'But you will dance with me again?'

Her heart skipped a beat. 'Tonight, yes, but I'll be gone tomorrow.'

'You're performing in Mexico City next month, aren't you?'

She swallowed. 'You'll be there?'

'Perhaps.'

She thought he wouldn't. Not once he'd had time to realise how crazy it was for someone like him to pursue a girl who had attracted him dancing on the stage.

A slow pulse of moody music came as the band resumed its performance. Ricardo stood and held his hand out to her. She floated on to the dance-floor with him. There seemed no way she could stop herself. Miguel was right, she knew that. This was dangerous. She must not lock eyes with Ricardo as they moved in the dance. She felt his hand on her back and the heat of his body only inches away from her. If he stepped closer without giving her room to retreat she would be crushed against his maleness.

She did not want that intimacy, yet she was powerless to stop her motion to the music in his arms. If his hand had moved in a caress on her back she might have broken the bond that locked their gazes, but he held her very correctly with no attempt to deepen the embrace... only his eyes... and the heat that stained her face and the flesh everywhere on her body.

'It's cooler on the balcony,' he murmured. He turned slightly and she saw that their dance had a purpose, that they were moving indirectly towards the open doors to the night air. As he turned again she caught a glimpse of another couple dancing through the open doors to the big balcony.

'I'm not warm,' she lied, staring up at him.

'I am.'

She swallowed, and his eyes took the motion so that she drew her lips between her teeth and gripped for an instant before she realised what she had done.

'If you intend to disappear on me,' he warned softly, 'I intend to kiss you before you go.'

One kiss. She had fantasised that as she waded in the water at the beach earlier. He had held her hand then...now her hand rested loosely in his as they danced.

'That balcony will be no different from the one at Señor Descanso's party,' she warned. 'I don't want...'

'Better than nothing,' he said, turning her with him in a swift sweep of motion that brought them closer to the night air. 'I told you I wanted you that night.'

'And I——'

His head bent down so that his voice was low and intense. 'You flamed at me with all the passion you hide when you put on your tourist costume.'

'This is the costume,' she whispered. 'This dress.'

He took her through the open doors and the coolness was a caress on her back.

'This is you,' he breathed against her hair. 'This is how I dream of you.'

Where had the other people gone? There had been others on the balcony earlier, but they were gone now. His face in her hair. Hand on her back. She tensed and pulled back until he released her from the dance embrace. Her hand fell against his chest. She stared at it and told it to move.

'We were dancing.' Her words were a whisper of growing panic. 'I wanted to dance, not this.'

'We will dance again.' The hand that had held hers was softly tangled in her hair. She didn't know if she tipped her head back or if he pulled it back. The fingers of his other hand cupped the curve of her cheek. She swallowed and felt the motion against his hand. Her breath went trembling out of her body and her tongue slipped out to wet her dry lips.

'What are you going to do?'

His fingers threaded through her hair, sending sensation tingling along her scalp. 'A kiss,' he reminded her. 'I'm going to kiss you as I've been aching to for days.'

'Only one kiss,' she pleaded. Only one for memories. She thought his lips would never begin the caress. He had both his hands in her hair now and she was trying to hold herself away from him but the slow movement of his mouth towards hers brought a sensation of dizziness that left her confused... her hands on his chest pressing to hold him away but lips parting because they must and thank God Miguel was just inside and he would come if she was out here much longer. Come and rescue her.

One kiss... before Miguel came... just one...

His lips were cool against hers. 'Close your eyes,' he whispered, but she stared into his eyes. His lips warmed her mouth with a touch softer than she'd known could come from a man. His eyelashes drooped so that she was staring at something in his face that made her breath seep out through parted lips.

Hands in her hair, slow caress that made her hair tingle over her back and stream through his hands and his whisper hoarse against her mouth. 'I love your hair. It's like you... all wild passion and temptation.'

'No...' The pulse beating in her chest spread. His lips teased her mouth. Her breath protested against his mouth and the touch of his kiss on the inner surface of her lower lip turned to a gasp she heard as it dragged into her lungs.

'Yes,' he whispered. 'I know, Maria...kiss me...'

She could feel her hair slipping between his fingers and her shoulders and his tongue stroking the place where her lips parted so that she could not press them closed and could not breathe enough to get words through her throat and her hands were flat on his chest, the only barrier to his body against hers. His heart was pounding hard against her palms, telling her what would be in the brown eyes if he lifted those long black lashes and let her see.

His fingers slid back up into her hair, taking the weight of her head so that she let it sag back and his lips were on her throat and she had to move but the pulse was heavier and mixed with the knowledge of an old nightmare was the pulsing anticipation she felt in the dance so that her body shuddered with ragged gulps of air as his hand slid down the long naked length of her back.

'*Dios, Maria*! What you do to a man!' Harsh words groaned against her throat...softness flooding away and his mouth hard against her lips, forcing...invading her darkly to take what he wanted.

She twisted and cried out but the sound was lost against his mouth. She couldn't breathe. His fingers clenched and her body convulsed. She jerked in panic but did not realise she had pulled free until his hands left her. Then air flooded into her lungs and jammed there.

She felt the coolness of stone against her back. The wall! Ricardo coming closer now, *that* look on his face and the way he moved like a panther about to claim prey and she was backed against the wall and nowhere to run but into his grip. He reached for her.

'I want...go in. I...'

'No games now,' he warned with a low growl. 'You want what I want. I felt your mouth parting for my kiss...your body trembling for my touch...'

The sound at her throat tried to be a word. His hand on her waist. Another hand on her hair and he was bringing her mouth to his, and it might have been a scream but it was locked and he took her mouth again and where the scream would have come was his mouth and his tongue and her body trembling and tensing both together.

No...

His mouth dragged away from hers. She felt her lips swollen with his passion and a great trembling started deep inside her but only his name got through her throat. His fingers traced down the soft tension of her neck where the words tried to get out and she tried to see him and there was nothing in front of her eyes. She was in his arms and suddenly he was too close against her with his voice whispering words she could not hear above her own heartbeat.

'Kiss me,' he growled. The echo told her he had demanded her kiss only seconds ago, his hands in her hair and his mouth on her face and her lips parted because for two pulses she knew again that this was Ricardo and it was the balcony where Miguel would come to save her from her own foolishness any second.

She became lost in his lips. Tongue, soft now, invading her mouth with the memory of the dance. Lips reminding her of the dream she'd denied and she whimpered and he stroked her back and said words she couldn't seem to hear.

His hands came together, sliding down the curve of her back. Possessing her hips and the wall against her back and his kiss lost the gentleness and passion snapped . . . the dance shattering against her body.

His body. Hard against hers.

Arms holding her. Trapping her. Nowhere to run and his voice gone . . . she fought and she couldn't breathe and it was the nightmare and she tried to cry out and she couldn't even seem to make the sound because the music was gone and silence now and the cry in her throat broken and his mouth hard against hers.

Her breath came back so suddenly that she was caught dragging in a hoarse cry of remembered horror. The night cold on her arms and her back. Hands hard on her arms. Voice low and snapping violently on her ears.

'Stop it! Maria!'

She gulped the sound inside.

'Open your eyes!'

Her eyes were closed in panic and she hadn't even known she had them squeezed tight against everything. She opened them. Dark shadow. Ricardo's shape. Her gaze flickered to her right. The doorway. People in there.

'If you run, I'll come after you.'

She froze. Her fingers clenched into her skirt.

'You're afraid,' he said grimly. 'You're terrified. Why in God's name didn't you tell me? Why let me think— did you think I would hurt you?'

She looked away from him. She swallowed twice and he was still waiting for an answer. 'Not exactly,' she whispered.

'Does your family know about this?'

The trembling wanted to take her over. Reaction. It was Ricardo in front of her. He'd kissed her but then the kiss had changed and she'd lost track of herself because this had happened so long ago and she hadn't known then the danger of smiling and letting the romantic dream unfold.

'Do your family know you're terrified to have a man touch you?'

'I'm not——'

He released his hold on her arms. Stepped back from her. 'You put on a hell of an act on that stage. A man looks at you and thinks you want the same thing he wants.'

'Let me go,' she begged. 'Please.'

He said nothing for a long time. Silence and she wanted to ask for her freedom again but she was afraid of the grimness she could see in his face.

She backed up when he stepped towards her.

'I promise you, Maria, that I will never hurt you.' He did not touch her with his hands or he would have felt her trembling. He bent his head and took her lips with his mouth. This time, he made no attempt to invade the trembling secrets of her mouth.

She swallowed when he stepped back, then gulped again. She wanted to look away from him but couldn't seem to do anything. Couldn't move. Couldn't talk. Could only shiver as if it were the cold north where she'd lived the year she was seventeen.

'Tomorrow you'll tell me what's behind this terror you feel,' he said.

Music from inside. She hadn't known the music had stopped but now it was there again and she heard it.

'No,' she said. 'Tomorrow I leave.' Inside were people. Maybe it was imagination but she could hear Miguel's voice talking and he would be dancing with a partner out on to this balcony soon. He'd arrange a change of partners and she would be safe again.

'Tomorrow morning,' Ricardo said grimly. 'Your plane leaves at noon and——'

'How do you know that?'

He brushed that aside with an angry gesture of his hand that made her shiver. 'If you don't meet me at nine in the restaurant of your hotel I'll be on that plane with you. I'll follow you, and when you change at Mexico City I'll be on that one too.'

He would follow her. It would be easy enough. Follow her from one flight to another. To her home where she had been safe. She had been a fool to think she was safe when she knew that this man thought of her as a temptation he did not want to resist. Hadn't she learned this bitter lesson well enough all those years ago when she'd run from Los Angeles?

'Maria?'

'Yes,' she agreed. 'Tomorrow morning at nine.'

It was a lie, the gypsy's defence.

# CHAPTER SIX

'TIA MARI! Let's swim back!'

'OK!' agreed Maria as she caught her small niece's floating body against her. She reached up one hand to grasp the boarding ladder of the anchored cabin cruiser. Encased in a life-jacket, Nita's body felt oddly bulky against her. 'Are you ready now? Or do you want to rest in the boat?'

'Swim,' voted Nita. Her black hair lay in wet ringlets all around her face. Nita's swimming skills were at the beginner level, but she loved to float in the life-jacket while her aunt swam at her side.

Maria gave her a quick hug. 'Right, then. *Vámonos*!' She turned on her back and swam slowly towards shore. Nita held on to one of Maria's hands and, half swimming and half towed along, she floated towards the shore.

They had been in the water every day since Maria's return from Mérida a week ago. During that time, Miguel's annoyance with his sister showed every time he looked at her. Insanity had struck her in Mérida. That was the only explanation. Miguel was right, she'd asked for it. Asked to be kissed wildly on the balcony of Los Arcos. Look at the way she'd danced with Ricardo, her gaze locked on his eyes boldly! Miguel had noticed, had warned her. And she'd known, for heaven's sake, that it was an invitation! Madness in her veins whispering that it didn't matter because it was the dance. Not real. Temptation because she knew he would take her lips on the balcony.

92

She'd danced out there with him. Knowing.

She'd been trapped into the dance with him at Señor Descanso's, but every step since then she had taken on her own. Why had she let him take her up on the ferris wheel? Why had she gone to meet him at the hot dog stand in the streets of Mérida during Mardi Gras? Why had she let him drive slowly past that policeman while he held her wrist to keep her prisoner and she didn't even cry out? If she'd wanted to be free, why hadn't she cried out?

She'd been uneasy, certainly, but she'd known when she went out to meet him that somehow he would persuade her to spend the day with him. And she'd gone with only nervousness, not fear. She'd let him hold her hand as they waded in the water at Progreso. She'd let her imagination play with the image of his kiss. When Miguel had offered her a sore ankle to avoid dancing with Ricardo, she'd pushed safety aside. She had danced in Ricardo's arms and held his eyes boldly while she'd dreamed of one kiss from his lips. *Dios*! He had seen that fantasy kiss in her eyes, and who could blame him for reading more than her silly dream?

Miguel was disgusted with her. She didn't blame him. He'd watched her dance with Ricardo and even he had thought she wanted to be alone on the balcony with Ricardo. And the part of her that was the fool had wanted his kiss until the instant when terrifying memories had broken over the innocent dream.

She'd known what Ricardo wanted from the beginning. He'd wanted a love-affair with the gypsy he believed to be passionate and sensual. Other men had wanted that, but Maria had never been caught by their desires before.

La Gitana. The gypsy would know how to play the part of Ricardo Swan's lover. She would sing for him. She would meet him in romantic candlelit rendezvous. She would dance as they had danced that last night at Los Arcos.

Mexico City next month. He would be there.

No, he wouldn't. Not now. Not when he found she had not kept her promise to meet him that next morning in Mérida. Not when he went to the desk and discovered that she and her brother had checked out in the middle of the night.

Miguel had been furious with her when she had burst into his room at three in the morning and begged him to spirit them away before morning. Away to another airport where Ricardo would not be able to put his threat into action.

'He'll be there, at the airport,' she had said desperately. 'He'll follow us and he'll find me.' She'd heard her voice rising and seen Miguel's face grim in front of her.

'*Cálmate, chica*. What can he do? I'll be with you. You are being *ilógica*. I'll talk to Dr Swan.'

'No!' She panicked at the thought of Miguel talking to Ricardo. Miguel had done that for her a few times in the past, when men had looked at her and not realised that standing alone on stage did not mean she was alone off stage. She had brothers. Protection.

'A kiss?' Miguel had demanded. 'He kissed you on the balcony? No more?'

'No more,' she agreed. She thought of Ricardo's hands holding her body against his. The sensation of his desire hard against her body and the memory of a nightmare.

'What did he do to frighten you?' Miguel demanded.

'Nothing.' The fear had come up from inside herself, swamping her with old horrors. 'Just a...a kiss. I——'

The thunder rose in Miguel's face. 'He forced you to accept his kiss?'

She gulped. 'No.'

'Then what?' He spread his hands in a gesture of frustration. 'Maria—*chica*, you like him. I know you do. I saw you dancing. And during dinner—your eyes never left him. He is attracted to you and he danced with you on to the balcony. An innocent kiss and you want to run away in the night. *Chica*——'

'Please, Miguel! Please—I know it was my fault.' She'd invited a kiss with that last dance. She might as well have taken out an advertisement telling him that she wanted his arms around her and his mouth buried in the softness of hers...that was what her eyes had promised. She knew they had. She'd felt it, dancing. But the dance wasn't supposed to escape into reality.

'One day you'll have to face this,' Miguel said finally. 'Or do you wish to be aunt to my children and live with no child of your own all your life? No husband.'

'A wife is not what he wants,' Maria snapped.

Miguel had grinned. 'Perhaps not, but he will realise that Maria Concerta is only possible for him as a wife.'

'No! I don't want a husband. I know you and Mamá think it is the only thing for a woman, but I have a career, Miguel. Your children are all I need of babies—and Emilio's, because some girl will trap him soon. Señorita Descanso perhaps.'

He had laughed then, because Emilio had already told them he was remaining in Mérida for a few days more. And although Miguel thought she was crazy he had

agreed to set off with her in a taxi in the middle of the
night so that she could escape Ricardo.

She'd escaped her own foolishness. She hadn't thought
she could be tempted by a man but now she knew there
was a danger. It would never happen again. She would
know better next time.

Nita pulled out of Maria's grip. 'Tia Mari? Who's that
man?' She pointed behind Maria, towards the shore.

Maria scrambled to find her footing on the sand under
the water. A man. She knew before she turned. She could
feel his gaze on her. Ricardo. Standing on the sand at
the edge of the water. Wearing pale tan trousers and a
matching short-sleeved silk shirt open at the neck. His
black hair was brushed to tameness and his hands were
pushed into the pockets of his trousers as if he'd been
walking that way. Strolling the beach.

She went two steps shallower in the water and stopped.

'Hello, Maria. *Cómo estás*?'

'Ricardo...'

She wasn't sure if his name actually got past her lips.
She could feel Nita splashing at her side and put her
hand on to the girl's shoulder. She didn't want to come
out of the water with him watching. She was wearing
nothing more than the black bathing suit. Bare arms and
legs and the low-cut bodice of the black suit. She took
another step and her thighs came free of the water. The
legs of the suit were high-cut. In California it would be
a conservative suit.

'Nita——' Her voice was slightly hoarse, perhaps from
the mouthful of water she'd swallowed when an unexpected wave slapped against her face earlier. 'Nita, this
is Dr Swan.'

She heard her niece's voice as from a distance. Then
Ricardo's, with the words making sound but no sense.

# TAKE 4 LOVE ON CALL ROMANCES FREE

*Mills & Boon Love on Call romances capture all the excitement, intrigue and emotion of a busy medical world. But a world never too busy to ignore love and romance.*

We will send you four Love on Call romances plus a cuddly teddy and a mystery gift absolutely FREE, as your introduction to this superb series.

At the same time we'll reserve a subscription for you to our Reader Service. Every month you could receive the latest four Love on Call romances delivered direct to your door postage and packing FREE, plus our FREE Newsletter packed with author news, competitions, special offers and much more.

What's more, there's no obligation. You may cancel or suspend your subscription at any time. So you've nothing to lose and a whole world of romance to gain!

## YOUR GIFT

Return this card today and we'll send you this lovely cuddly teddy bear absolutely FREE.

*Fill in the Free Books Certificate overleaf* ▶ ▶

# Free Books Certificate

**Yes!** Please send me four FREE Love on Call romances together with my FREE cuddly teddy and mystery gift. Please also reserve a special Reader Service subscription for me. If I decide to subscribe, I shall receive four brand new books every month for just £7.20, postage and packing FREE. If I decide not to subscribe, I shall write to you within 10 days. Any free books and gifts will be mine to keep in any case. I understand that I am under no obligation whatsoever – I may cancel or suspend my subscription at any time simply by writing to you. I am over 18 years of age.

## Your Extra Bonus Gift

We all love mysteries, so as well as the books and cuddly teddy we've an intriguing gift just for you. No clues – send off today!

Ms/Mrs/Miss/Mr _____ 1A4D

Address _____

_____

_____

Postcode _____ Signature _____

**Mills & Boon
Reader Service
FREEPOST
PO Box 236
Croydon
CR9 9EL**

▶ **Send No Money Now**

Ricardo bent down and Nita was standing in front of him while he unfastened her life-jacket. As if she were one of the nieces he'd mentioned.

Maria crossed to where she'd spread a blanket in the sand earlier. She picked up her terry wrap and belted it around herself. It wasn't enough covering, but at least when he stood from helping Nita there was nothing for him to look at but the length of her tanned legs.

Nita pulled on his arm. 'Do you live in Los Cabos?' she asked him in Spanish.

'No,' he said, smiling down at her. 'It's my first time here. I came to see your aunt Maria.'

'*Está bien*,' said Nita with a grin. 'She's nice, isn't she?'

'I think she's angry with me.' His eyes challenged Maria.

Nita bit her lip. 'Don't worry, Dr Swan. If she gets angry with you—you just tell her you love her and she smiles again.'

Ricardo laughed and Maria could feel the heat in her cheeks. She shook her head in denial but the curls were all wet ringlets around her face. She combed her fingers through them.

'Nita, go to the house and tell Papá we have company.'

Ricardo looked thoughtful as he watched Nita run up towards the house with the life-jacket trailing from her hand. Maria felt her heart beating somewhere below the place where a heart should be.

'Sending for reinforcements?' he asked.

'Yes.' There didn't seem much point in denying it. 'I didn't think you would follow me.'

He shook his head sharply. 'Don't lie, Maria. Not to me. You knew.'

A man, Nita had said, and Maria had known it was Ricardo come to her again.

'Is that Miguel's job?' he asked. 'To keep lovers away from you?'

'Yes,' she whispered. 'He's my brother. He's always——'

'You ran away.'

She didn't know what to say. The gypsy might have challenged his right to come, but the gypsy wasn't here in this place. On this beach there was only Maria the woman. She could see heat from the sun in his face. His eyes were narrowed and his mouth bracketed with frown lines. No smile now.

'Why did you follow me?'

He slid his hands out of his pockets. 'You know why.'

She backed up a half-step and combed one hand through her wet hair. 'I—after what happened in Mérida... You must realise that I don't want you to——'

'Seduce you?' He stepped towards her. She backed away.

His hand reached out to touch her lips. A soft touch...featherlight on her mouth...drawing a memory of his lips on hers.

'I want you, Maria Concerta. What are we going to do about that?'

She should pull back...step back...break free of that gentle touch. But she was held by the look on his face. She wasn't sure if it was the desire she'd seen when he watched her dance... or something else she'd never let herself see before.

'Nothing.' Her voice sounded frighteningly small. 'We aren't going to do anything about it.'

His touch slid away across her mouth, hesitated at the vulnerable pulse of her throat. 'Are you sure that's what you really want? Nothing?'

Just memories. One kiss that echoed in her dreams and in her pulse when she practised the new songs in the music room of her family home. She had woken from the dream least night with the knowledge that while she slept Ricardo had touched her in ways she had read in books of love. Only a dream.

'I have to go and——' She pulled away from his touch. 'Nita—I told Ana I would look after——'

'Maria, stop.'

She froze, half turned away from him.

'Don't run,' he said. 'Your brother will be here soon enough.'

'This is crazy,' she whispered. She wrapped her arms around her midriff, pressing the terry cloth of her wrap close to her flesh. 'You're crazy to come here. If you come close I'll run. I don't want this.'

He shook his head sharply. 'You're afraid. I understand that now, although you've yet to tell me——'

'No!' She gulped. 'You want the gypsy singer. She isn't real. I made her up.'

He reached for her and she felt his hands on her arms through the terry cloth. Gentle and firm. His face was sober. For a second she thought he was going to kiss her and she realised that her own lips had parted in the crazy betrayal that made no sense at all.

'Ric——'

'Listen to me!' His fingers tightened on her arms. 'Understand this . . . and do not forget it.' His words had become heavily accented as if with emotion held back. 'There would never be pleasure for me in touching you...' his hands released their grip and his palms brushed down along the length of her upper arms '...no pleasure unless you wanted my touch as much as I wanted to give it.'

'No, I don't! Why did you come after me?'

'Because I know that you wanted my kiss when I danced with you that last night...and earlier, on the beach.'

She stared at the bulk of white terry that was her own folded arms, Ricardo standing in front of her and her arms folded like a barrier between them.

'Yes,' she admitted. Her voice sounded faint.

'Tell me why you're afraid.'

She tilted her head back so that she was staring at him through narrowed eyes. 'Do you see me as a mystery? Is that why you came? Your passion for the hidden truth?' She was trembling all through herself and her voice was rising. 'Do you need to probe me like the dust around Mérida? And you——'

'Stop it!' He shook her sharply, hands holding her arms, then released her. His eyes flickered past her. 'Your brother is coming now. Does that make you feel safer?'

She shivered. It should but it didn't.

'Will you use him to run from me again?'

'Yes,' she whispered.

'Maria?' Miguel's voice called out harsh behind her.

She sucked in a deep breath. Ricardo had her locked in his gaze and if she turned away...

'Señor Swan?' challenged Miguel's voice. Claiming territory. His sister. Maria saw Ricardo's head lift slightly as he accepted the challenge.

'Señor Concerta,' he acknowledged. 'It's a pleasure to see you again.'

'Unexpected,' said Miguel.

They were speaking in Spanish. Formally. Polite voices and she could feel the tension but she heard the politeness like a rein on both men. Miguel touched her shoulder.

'Go up to the house, Maria. You'll get cold.'

In the heat of the afternoon sun they all knew that was ridiculous, yet she was shivering and could not stop the trembling that consumed her. Miguel had come to protect her but the danger was inside her own self.

She didn't want Ricardo here. *She didn't want him to leave either.*

'Señor Concerta?' Ricardo's voice was abruptly demanding. 'Leave us, *por favor*. Maria and I must speak alone.'

'About what?' Miguel demanded.

A muscle jerked along the side of Ricardo's jaw. 'I've come to ask your sister to be my wife.'

'No,' she whispered. She felt Miguel's hand drop away from her shoulder. She turned and saw her brother's gaze narrowed in a warning as he stared at Ricardo.

'You will come to the house when you have talked with my sister?'

'*Sí*,' agreed Ricardo.

'No,' Maria said.

'You will stay to dinner,' said Miguel.

Ricardo inclined his head.

'I will watch the beach from the house,' said Miguel without expression.

'*Sí*,' agreed Ricardo. 'I understand.'

As if they were negotiating! Handing her over from Miguel Concerta Sanchez to Dr Ricardo Swan...as if she were a chattel! She lifted her head high and made her hands into fists.

'Miguel! You listen to me! I am marrying no one!'

'*Chica*, it is time you talked to him.'

She could feel a pulse beating behind her temple and knew that she might scream, that she might say anything. Miguel would leave and she would be here alone with Ricardo and he would not do more than perhaps another kiss here on the open beach with the house looking down...but...

She felt a lurch deep in her chest. 'Yes,' she agreed. 'I'll talk.'

Miguel turned away. She watched him walk up the path to the *casa*. She pushed her hands into the pockets of her wrap and chewed on her lip.

'Are you cold?' asked Ricardo.

She shook her head. She turned away from the safety of the house and walked down towards the water. Perhaps there was no safety with Miguel, but if she needed to get away she would swim out. Swim steadily deeper until she was at the cruiser. He wouldn't follow fully dressed. She looked back and he was three paces behind her. A man who did not give up. She pushed her hands deeper into the pockets.

'Why did you say that to Miguel? You don't want to marry me.'

'What would you have me tell him?' His lips twisted into a rueful smile. 'That I cannot sleep for dreaming of you in my bed?'

His eyes told her what he might say. 'I want to have your sister for my lover. I will visit her in Mexico City and Cancún and Monterey and I will take her in my arms and touch my lips to hers...stroke her trembling soft flesh until she is as wild as the heart that dances...'

He saw it. His eyes took the words of the fantasy from her mind.

'Not...marriage. I'll never give anyone that power over me.'

'Will you be my lover?'

She turned her head away sharply. 'I can't.'

His hand took her closed fist. 'Walk with me, then.'

He set the pace, moving slowly. They walked away from the sun. 'How long have you lived here?' he asked.

'Eight years. My father and Miguel bought it after I came back from the States.'

'Los Angeles?'

'Yes.' She stepped ahead of him but his hand did not release hers.

'Why were you in Los Angeles?'

She shrugged and kicked the sand with one bare foot. When she glanced up at him he was very tall because she was not wearing heels. It would be easier, she thought, if he were a smaller man. If he did not make her so aware of her helplessness should he use strength against her.

'Do you have relatives up there?'

'My father's sister lives there with her husband. I stayed with them to finish my high school.' She shrugged with studied casualness. 'It was a long time ago.'

'And you returned—when?'

She pulled her hand away. 'Why should you ask all the questions?'

He touched her cheek to brush away a damp curl. 'Because you are a mystery.'

'Some mysteries you must leave unsolved.'

'Why did you scream when I was kissing you?'

'I didn't——' A muscle clenched deep in her stomach. '*Dios*! Did anyone hear?'

'No. My mouth was on yours.'

She flushed at the memory. Sensations and dreaming and tension building until the terror of the past flooded over her . . . his body hard against her and if he had not covered the scream with his kiss the whole of Los Arcos would have heard.

'It's the gypsy you wanted.' Her voice trembled. 'The...passionate woman. I tried to tell you she's not real.'

His hand brushed aside her words. 'Will you tell me why you are frightened?'

'I—I can't.'

'I could ask your brother.' He looked back the way they had come.

'No!' She reached out and grabbed the soft silk of his shirt. 'He won't tell you!'

'He knows?'

'Can't we stop this?' The silk was crushed in her fist. She released it and made a blind gesture with her hand. 'Don't you have to be somewhere? Ecuador or Los Angeles or Mérida?'

'Toronto,' he said. 'I've just come from there. Otherwise I'd have been here sooner.'

'Why Toronto?' She swallowed the question. 'Why—I wish you'd go back.'

'Do you, Maria?' He smiled then. 'I think we must marry. I can hardly seduce you under your brother's watchful eyes.'

'You could give up. Go away.'

'No.'

She made a sound of derision. 'Will you force me to the priest? Force the *sí* from my throat when he asks me if I will have you?' She pulled away, walked ahead of him and tossed her words back on the wind. 'If you want La Gitana, come to my performance in Mexico City next month. She'll be there. On stage.'

'She is here as well.'

'No!' She spun to face him. Three metres between them and he could cross that sand in a second. 'You want me for something that isn't there. You're crazy— *loco*!'

'Yes,' he agreed. 'A crazy man. But it is you I want, not the woman on the stage. The gypsy in your heart is much more dangerous than the woman on stage.' He reached out to touch the air as if it were her flesh. 'To watch a hesitant flush on your cheek, then a moment later to see your head go up and your voice come alive with the passion that is in your blood. As if you would try to deny that passion we both know is there.'

'There's nothing!' Her shout echoed on the wind.

His gaze slid slowly down the bulky terry cloth that concealed her flesh. 'Do you think passion is only in lovemaking?' he demanded softly. 'I thought that when I first saw you. You mesmerised me . . . I wanted to leave Mérida the next day because I knew that if I stayed——'

'You should have left.' They were glaring at each other like bull and bullfighter in the ring. She muttered, 'If I've cast a spell on you, then get away! Get over it.'

'Get over you?' Mockery flicked around his voice, as if he was amused by his own passions. He slid his hands into the pockets of his trousers and looked out over the water towards the birds that circled high and far out to sea. 'In the beginning,' he said slowly, 'I told myself that I would taste your passion and be myself again.' He turned his head back towards her. Then he moved. She told herself to run, but when he took her face in his hands she trembled and was still as he stared down into her eyes.

'Do you think I would hurt you?'

She swallowed.

'I know you're afraid.' His thumbs caressed her cheeks. 'Yet when I look into your eyes . . . I see that you also want this . . .'

His mouth came to hers so slowly that she could not make herself feel the danger. She stared up and saw the hard lines around his mouth soften and blur. Then his lips settled on to hers. Softly. Gently. Then gone and he released her. She stared up at his eyes dark and probing on hers.

'Will you tell me what happened to you?'

She could not answer.

'One day you will tell me,' he said gently.

'I—don't know.'

A muscle flickered in his jaw. 'I know it was in Los Angeles. When you talk about living there, that's where the shadow is.'

She put her hands in front of her, between them as if to ward him off. He tangled the fingers of both her hands with both his. She stared at his strong brown fingers linked with hers. Her gaze flickered up to his face and he too was studying their linked hands. She felt the spin of unreality as if she were dancing back in Mérida and her gaze was locked on his eyes throughout the dance.

He looked up at her and his eyes were deep and very dark.

'I don't want to frighten you, Maria, but you must see that if I don't know what happened——'

She touched her lower lip with her tongue. 'You're not going away?'

'No.'

'I won't marry you. That's . . . crazy.' She grimaced slightly.

'We'll be lovers with a marriage or without.' He said the words as if it made little difference which. 'But you've got to admit that seducing you is going to be a bit of a challenge with your brother breathing fire all over the place.'

She felt a hysterical bubble of laughter in her throat. 'How can you seduce a woman who doesn't want to be... seduced?' How could she stand here between the sand and the water with his hands holding hers while they talked about seduction?

'I know the woman does like kissing me.' He was closer now and she could feel what was coming in the tension from his hands and the message from his eyes. 'I've kissed her twice now and...'

'And?' Her hands were gripping his. Standing so close to him and if he kissed her again she would feel the touch of his tongue probing the tenderness of her lower lip and she would let her eyes drift closed and...

'And I'm sure she enjoys kissing. Doesn't she, Maria?'

She touched her lower lip with her tongue. He released one of her hands and stroked her cheek with light fingertips. She felt her eyes go wide as she stared up at him.

'This seduction,' he said slowly, 'will proceed more smoothly if the lady being seduced doesn't lie to...'

'To her seducer?' she breathed.

'To her lover. Do you want me to kiss you, Maria?'

She tried to say a word. No... or yes. There was only a husky breath that might be either invitation or panic. 'Ricardo, this won't work. I don't——'

He pressed his fingers against her lips to silence her. 'That wasn't the question. Right now we're talking only about a kiss.' His words trailed along the surface of her skin with a tremble in their wake.

A kiss. She lifted her hand up and closed her fingers around his wrist to take his touch away from her mouth. Did she want...did she want him to kiss her again?

Yes. If it could be safe.

He broke the clasp of her fingers and linked his hand with hers again.

'I was supposed to go to the University of Southern California,' she said abruptly. 'The School of Music. After I graduated.' She stared at his chest...the second button on his shirt. The buttons were slightly darker than the tan colour of the shirt itself. 'My father believed that I could train for a career in classical music. I used to sing with him but he stopped that when I was thirteen. He said I must go to the States to train.'

She tried to pull back but he kept her hands. He didn't say anything. If he had, she might not have been able to say more. Or if she had to look into his face while she spoke.

'I had a voice teacher while I was taking my last year of high school. Private lessons.' His thumbs stroked the backs of her hands. She swallowed and forced the words to go on. 'Then in...in April she had an accident and an ex-student of hers took over teaching her students.'

She looked up and the words disappeared.

'What was the new teacher's name?'

'Wallace——' Something flared in Ricardo's eyes and she didn't say the rest of the name. 'He liked my voice. He—I had lessons two evenings a week and—and——' His hands tightened on hers. 'He was...very nice to me. Very...handsome and it was——' She gulped. 'It was work before, with Miss Stanners, but when Wallace took over it—he made it fun and I looked forward to—and I guess I——' Her breath had all gone out with the words. Why was she telling this dismal story? She didn't even let herself *think* about this! Why bring it back with words?

'You fell in love with him.'

She nodded, staring at that button on his shirt, wondering what she could hear in his voice? Disgust? Anger? Boredom? 'Yes,' she said finally. 'I fell in love with him.'

'Maria! Look at me!'

She lifted her chin. His brows were thick and heavy, bunched up together so that she could not read his eyes. She wasn't going to cry. No matter what.

'How old was he?'

She shrugged and pulled at his hands but he shook his head slightly.

'Twenty-eight,' she muttered. 'About.'

'What happened?'

She shivered. ''I—he said it was my fault.'

She heard his breath hiss. 'Just say it, Maria.'

'I—don't know if——' She gulped. 'Summertime. I— I had lessons three times a week in the afternoons. At his studio. I was—he asked me once if I wanted to go to the beach with him afterwards and I—I brought my suit the next day and——' She bit her lip and it was her hands now gripping his. 'We went to the beach where the surfers were and...and he kissed me.'

She couldn't look at Ricardo. He was waiting and she said it all quickly because it would be over then and he'd let go of her hands and she could have peace because he would go away.

'He—the next week, after the beach. He said...sort of a celebration because he'd been coaching me for my audition for the music school and—and I'd been accepted.' Her heart was thundering. She knew where her own words were going and dreaded it. A dream and she was walking on and on towards the ending.

Ricardo's thumbs rubbing the back of her hands. Strength or anger. She didn't know which, could not look into his face to find out. 'I—I knew my aunt and uncle wouldn't think—they would think he was too old. My aunt was pretty American and I had dated a little but you see—I said I was going to the show with a girlfriend. I met him——' She dragged in air. 'I met him outside his studio at ... at six.'

She gulped and Ricardo's hands were gripping hers too tightly but he was still stroking the backs of her hands with his thumbs, and she was staring at the second button on his shirt as if something terrible might happen if she let it out of her sight.

'I thought he was taking me to a restaurant. I thought he would dance with me and maybe he would kiss me again.'

'Maria...'

Her hands clenched when he released them. He slid his hands up along her arms and she realised that she was shaking...trembling everywhere, not just her voice.

'Romantic,' she whispered. 'I thought—that's what I thought—I——'

'I know.' His voice was neutral, too quiet. 'Romantic, like your songs ... like the dance?'

'Yes,' she whispered. 'But he drove to—not a restaurant—a house on the beach. A friend's, he said. I didn't—I didn't know what to do... He'd said dinner and when I—he said what difference did it make whether the dinner was in a restaurant or by the beach and we could ... could ta—talk without——'

He shook her slightly. A sob broke in her throat and he cursed softly. 'Enough! I understand well enough what happened. I won't make you say it.'

She gulped. 'He said——' she shook her head but could not seem to stop the words now they had started '—it was my fault. He said the way I walked—the way I'd looked at him—that I should expect—should have known——'

'Stop this!' His hands gripped tightly. 'You were hardly more than a child!'

Without his hands holding her she thought she might slip down into the sand. 'But I—I knew he was watching me. I—you said—in Mérida you told me yourself that when I walked——'

He grasped her chin roughly. 'Maria! Look at me!'

She could feel the tension in him but the anger in his eyes was masked. Anger concealed and therefore more dangerous. 'I have three sisters,' he said grimly. 'They've all been in love at sixteen or seventeen with a teacher or a movie star. An older man they fantasised about.' His jaw went rigid as a convulsion of tension gripped him. 'My sisters are all beautiful women...as you are a beautiful woman. Because a woman is beautiful and she moves like a woman...and she's a little in love with a man she doesn't really know——' He jerked his head. 'Nothing excuses a man using his strength against a woman. *Nunca*! Never!'

She breathed in and tried to get something over the emotions coming loose but the tears were coming unless she could flood them out with anger or laughter.

'You were a child! Only a child!' Anger blazed in his eyes now. 'Your Wallace was old enough to know exactly what he was doing.' His face was harsh, frightening. 'If I ever——' The fire in his eyes blazed and disappeared and she saw his face freeze into a mask of tension that concealed the anger.

She moistened the dryness of her lips with her tongue. Her lips parted but she didn't know what to say. She wanted to get away, to be alone. That was how she would end. Alone, because when his anger was gone he would look at her differently. She shrugged again and whispered, 'So you see——'

He was staring at his own hands as they slowly released her. 'What should I see?'

'That there's no point to this.' She wished she had a stage role to call on now, but she didn't know any gypsy image that would make it easier to stand in front of him in her bare feet on the beach after what she'd just told him.

# CHAPTER SEVEN

MARIA knew that she had to stop what was happening, but each hour the tide Ricardo had started seemed to thicken around her.

She hadn't said yes. She had not said either to Ricardo or to her family that she was willing to marry Ricardo. Yet everyone around her behaved as if a wedding between Maria Concerta and Ricardo Swan was inevitable. She felt as if she were moving on stage without knowing the story. She was stuck in a terrible mire where she couldn't seem to say anything at all.

Ricardo hadn't said anything *to* her since her confession on the beach. He knew it was impossible, so why was he still here? Why was he talking with Miguel about his family in Ecuador and his business interests in Canada, his own home in the States—as if he was giving Miguel the information a girl's older brother had a right to ask for? As if he intended this marriage to happen.

Mamá was planning the wedding. *The wedding*!

'April,' Mamá said at the dinner-table that first night. 'April is a good time for the wedding. Right after Maria performs in Mexico City, because it's too late to cancel Mexico City, isn't it, Miguel?'

Miguel agreed that La Gitana had no choice but to appear in Mexico City for the scheduled concert and recording sessions.

'And do we keep all this a secret?' asked Emilio, who had just returned from Mérida. 'Or do we throw the event to the media? La Gitana and her——!'

113

'It will be a private wedding,' said Ricardo. At once everyone agreed. And Miguel——!

Miguel, who had been her manager ever since Papá got sick—Miguel asked Ricardo's advice about the new record contract! Maria couldn't believe it! She knew she had to stop this! The longer it went on, the harder it would be for her to assert herself. Yet it all seemed like a crazy dream. Mamá and Ana insisted that Ricardo must check out of his hotel in San José del Cabo and come to stay at their *casa*. Mamá gave him the big guest room on the third storey. Maria slept on the second storey, between Nita's room and Emilio's.

Ricardo Swan. Maria Concerta's *novio*.

He was always near. Talking to Miguel. Taking them out in the car he'd rented in San José. Talking to her brothers, who both seemed to accept him as if *he'd* been their older brother for years.

He couldn't possibly mean this wedding to happen. She had no idea what it was he intended, except that he wasn't leaving. He moved into the *casa* on Thursday, the day after that shattering conversation on the beach. On Friday he took Maria and Nita into San José del Cabo and it was a strange trip. He hardly spoke to her at all, and she didn't talk to him. They spoke to Nita.

Saturday there was a big barbecue at the Concerta *casa*. Friends who had been invited some time ago. The fire burning down on the beach and chairs everywhere and all the women sitting on one side in cotton dresses with full skirts, talking and laughing, and the men on the other side of the fire in short sleeves and dress trousers.

Everyone teased Maria. She moved among them all as if it were a rehearsal for a performance. They all toasted Maria and Ricardo and she felt the scream crawling up into her throat and Ricardo watching her as if he wondered when she would stand up and deny it all. Was that why he stayed? Because he was an honourable man and he'd told her brother he would marry her. So *she* must be the one to publicly deny the union.

'Maria,' said Ana softly the next morning.

'Yes?'

Ana was a shy woman, quiet and most content at home with her husband and child. Now she smiled at her sister-in-law and asked, 'What will you do after you marry Ricardo? You won't perform, will you?'

Maria's lips parted on a denial.

'I hope you'll quit,' said Ana before Maria's words form.

'Why?'

'Miguel could stay home.' Ana flushed. '*Estoy embarazada*,' she confessed, touching her waist. 'Another baby, and Miguel promised me that this time he would try not to be travelling so much through my time. But I know he won't let you go alone on tour.'

Maria hadn't realised that Miguel's travelling with her was causing a problem between him and Ana. Miguel had managed her career for so long she had no idea how she could manage without him. He and Ana loved each other deeply, but Maria knew Ana hated the travelling although when Nita was younger she had sometimes come with them on the road.

'And Nita,' said Ana. 'She goes to school this year. Her *papá* should be near.'

'Don't worry,' she said to Ana. 'It will be all right. You'll see.'

Maria had the feeling her life was coming apart from the inside out. Whatever happened between her and

Ricardo—when Ricardo finally went out of her life, this problem of Ana's desire to have Miguel at home would still be there.

They went to church on Sunday, as always. Ricardo sat at her side through the service. Each time she knelt or stood during the service, she was aware of his body moving in concert with hers. She kept her eyes on the priest and the choir, but she could see Ricardo's arms out of the corner of her eye. She felt even the quietest breath he took. When they sang hymns his voice was deep and strong, its timbre echoing in her pulse. She could see the back of Nita's head in the pew in front of her. With the music and Ricardo's voice and the fabric of his suit brushing against her arm, for a spinning moment she thought that Nita was hers and Ricardo's and it was all real.

What if she couldn't get her voice to say a word of protest and he really meant it? What if April ended and she had a ring on her finger and Ricardo took her away from her home and she was trapped as his possession forever? She didn't know why she couldn't scream out a protest. This was her family. Miguel whom she'd argued with and relied on all her life. Emilio whom she'd laughed with. Mamá who loved her but could never understand why Maria didn't dream of a husband of her own. Ana who loved Nita and Miguel and the peace of their home.

Her family. All she had to do was make them understand she didn't want a wedding. Surely Ricardo didn't want a wedding either? Surely if she waited—surely Ricardo would find some graceful way to get them both out of this.

By the time the weekend was over, she had learned a lot about him, mostly from listening to the others talking with him. Two of his three sisters lived in Ecuador. The eldest was married and her husband managed the family business in Ecuador. Ricardo was also connected with that business, although Maria didn't ask him how. She didn't want to collect details about his life. She overheard him answering her mother's questions about his family. It was the things that Ricardo didn't say about the family business that told her there was a great deal of wealth. Oil wells, and a school that had been established to help the peasants adjust to the changing reality of Ecuador as it moved into the twenty-first century.

His business in Toronto was related to mining. Maria overheard that when Emilio asked Ricardo if they spoke French in Toronto. Later she walked past the open doorway to Miguel's study and heard the man everyone thought she was going to marry saying casually that he was on a two-year sabbatical from the university and doubted if he would return except as a guest lecturer.

This was ridiculous! Everyone had pieces of Ricardo's life, while *she*, the woman he'd said he was marrying, knew almost nothing except that he'd lusted after her until he found out who she really was.

She had to stop this. The sooner the better.

Ana had planned to take Nita to the market in San José del Cabo on Monday to look for fabric for a doll's dress. But at breakfast on Monday it was obvious that Ana was feeling ill.

'Morning sickness,' she whispered to Maria.

'I'll take Nita into town,' Maria offered. 'Emilio and I are taking a day off practice in any case.'

'I'll drive you,' offered Ricardo.

She turned around to face him. Ana was leaving the dining-room and the others hadn't come in yet. Just her and Ricardo standing only inches apart, and it was the first time they'd been completely alone since that time on the beach.

'Ricardo, I must talk to you.' Her breath packed up in her throat. It was silly to be afraid, but looking up at him and planning to tell him how crazy all this was——

'Past time,' he agreed. 'We'll talk this afternoon.'

When Maria moved to follow Nita, Ricardo stopped her with a hand on her arm.

They were at the ice-cream stand in the village. Ricardo had just given Nita the money to pay for an ice-cream cone. Nita had stepped up to the counter to say she wanted pistachio flavoured, 'And a *doble*, not a single,' she insisted.

'I'll go with her,' Maria said, pulling against Ricardo's hand. 'To be sure——'

'She doesn't need help. You wanted to talk to me?'

'Yes.' She wasn't sure what she'd intended to say.

'I asked you once if you were afraid of me.' His hand moved against her shoulder, stroking it lightly. 'You didn't answer.'

She looked away from him. Nita was standing at the counter on her toes, talking to the ice-cream girl.

'Maria?'

'I wish you would stop trying to——' She swallowed a confusion of words because she was no longer certain just what it was that he hoped to win from her. 'You can't actually plan to marry me,' she whispered.

'Can't I?'

'I won't marry you.'

'When April comes,' he said quietly, 'we'll know the truth of that.'

'You don't mean to go on with this?'

'Don't I?'

Even as she read the anger in his face, it was gone. 'You're—you're angry?'

'I read your thoughts on your face.' His smile was mocking. 'What is it you want to say to me, Maria? "Go away, Ricardo? I want you to leave me"?' The smile that came to his lips made her shiver. 'Those are the words that tremble on your lips, but in your eyes I see another truth. Don't tell me to leave, Maria. Not unless it's truly your desire.'

She gulped. 'It's—I——'

'If you want me to abandon you, you'd be screaming—throwing things at any member of your family who said there would be a wedding. Admit that at least.' His face was sober, the lines deep on either side of his mouth.

She turned away from him. 'I don't know why I haven't said—— We can't—can't marry!' Her voice rose and she gulped when she saw a woman on the pavement turn to stare. 'We can't!' she whispered fiercely. 'We're not in love and I won't—I couldn't——' She pressed her hands to her face to stifle the confusion.

'You are saying that you could never bring yourself to make love with me?' The question was hissed.

She closed her eyes and dropped her hands from her face. He was in her dreams. A dream echo of this man touching her in ways that made her face flame and her pulse beat in panic and yearning. 'Maybe...' She could not look at him but knew he would hear her words. 'Sometimes I think that we could be lovers. But not like this! I—I need time.'

'You have until April.' There was no more emotion in his face than she had heard in his voice.

'You're like a chameleon,' she muttered. 'What you think and feel turns on and off in your face.'

'Nita is coming back.' He took her arm and gestured her towards one of the tables. 'And you, Maria, are at the mercy of those feelings you refuse to acknowledge. If you want my thoughts and feelings, you know well enough how to prod them to the surface.'

'Where is this going?' she demanded breathlessly.

'Where do you want it to go?'

'I don't know!' She pulled away from him and sat in the chair facing the street. 'Will you stop playing with me?'

'The truth for once,' he muttered. 'If I leave you now—if I come to you in Mexico City in April—what then, Maria? Will you have your masks tightly in place again?'

'You mean—would I be your lover?'

'Yes.'

She swallowed. 'I don't know. Yes—maybe.'

He sighed. 'You would lie as easily as tell me the truth, and sometimes I wonder if you know the truth yourself. Do you want me to go away?'

Maria bit her lip and traced a design on the table. A few feet away the people of San José were walking past on their Monday business. Two tables away two gringa women were talking loudly in English.

'There isn't any point in your staying,' she said slowly. 'You wanted La Gitana. And I'm not her.'

He covered her hand. 'The last time we danced...'

She flushed.

'...you were the same woman I saw dance on the stage.'

'Miguel was very angry with me,' she whispered. 'I was pretending.'

'What were you pretending?'

She flushed. 'That it was safe.'

He leaned forward and cupped her face with his other hand. 'Maria, are you afraid of me? Of me specifically?'

She trembled. 'No. But——'

'Hush.' His fingers pressed against her lips. 'Hush, *chica*. That's enough for now.'

She jerked back from his touch. 'I won't have you hovering—waiting for a moment when I—I don't *want* the things you think of when you look at me like that.'

'What do you want, Maria? For the dance to be real?'

She covered her cheeks with her hands. 'Don't do that,' she whispered.

'When I kissed you—you wanted that to be real.'

She shook her hair back and felt the wind take it. She kept her eyes down as she combed her fingers through its length. 'When we danced—I thought—I thought a kiss would be safe.' She looked up at him then. 'I'm sorry,' she whispered. 'I know I let you think—but that was all I wanted.'

'I have no regrets,' he said softly, his eyes gentle. 'Only that I made you remember. One day I'll erase that painful memory from your heart forever.'

She looked around desperately. Nita at the counter. Ricardo's eyes on her and that promise and she'd forgotten even where they were. 'I'll go and see if Nita——' She pushed her chair back and he said something but she got away to where Nita was picking up the ice-cream cone. She couldn't bear to listen to his promises.

'One day I'll erase that painful memory... forever...' She kept hearing his voice say that. Over and over again. But how could you erase a nightmare?

They took Nita to the market where Ricardo studied the fabrics for the doll dress with such concentration that it might have been the most important decision in his day.

'The blue,' suggested Maria, but Ricardo had said he liked the pink and Nita would have nothing but the pink.

'It's going to clash horribly with the doll buggy Miguel has bought for her birthday,' Maria hissed to Ricardo. 'It's red.'

He laughed and swung Nita up on to his shoulder. 'Maybe your aunt is right,' he said confidentially to the little girl. 'My sisters tell me that I have no eye for colour. Why don't you have the blue?'

'The pink,' said Nita, and in the end it was the pink Maria told the merchant to cut a half-metre of, but Ricardo insisted on paying. Maria saw the merchant put the blue fabric in beside the pink. Ricardo had bought both for Nita.

On the way out of the market, Ricardo stopped them at the stand of an artisan selling hand-crafted jewellery. 'The jade,' he told the old man.

Maria stepped back sharply. The jade earrings. She'd looked at them a few moments ago. He had seen what she was thinking. He had known that of all the pieces here it was the jade earrings that attracted her.

'No,' she whispered.

But the earrings were in his hand and a sheaf of *pesos* disappeared into the artisan's pocket. The old man said to Ricardo, '*Bonita! La señorita!*'

She shook her head, staring at Ricardo. 'I don't want you to give me——'

'Shall I put them in your ears?'

'No,' she whispered, touching one ear with uneasy fingers. His hands would be careful against her flesh.

She could feel his touch as if he had indeed slipped her gold posts out of her ears and carefully replaced them with the jade earrings. Her breathing would break and...

He stepped towards her.

She held her hand out. 'Give them—give them to me!' She stepped back when he came another step closer but there was nowhere to go. There was a woman passing close behind her... Nita and Ricardo in front of her. 'Don't touch me!' she snapped.

'Are you afraid?' he demanded softly.

Nita laughed and pulled on Ricardo's arm. 'Tia Mari isn't afraid of anybody.'

Maria was panicked by the thing in her veins. The pulse. The restlessness. She fumbled with one earring and slipped the wire into her ear. The jade pendant swung against her flesh, caressing her. He would seduce her. He would be her lover with marriage or without. If she made him wait until they married then he would own more than her body.

'What did you do with the handbag you bought in Mérida?' she whispered.

'Will you accept it now?'

'You still have it?'

'Of course.'

She lifted her chin slightly, his gift of jade swinging against her skin. 'I sent your roses to the orphanage. Every day I sent them away.'

His eyes darkened. 'Don't give away the earrings.'

The pulse beat heavily in her when he watched her. What if she could not change his mind about this wedding? What if she couldn't find whatever it was that she needed to stop the inevitable...?

The restlessness grew on her through the rest of the day. Nita had to ask her several times if she thought the pink would make a pretty dress before she heard the question.

'It'll be fine,' she said. 'It's pretty.'

'You'll be married to Tia Mari by then, won't you?' demanded Nita of Ricardo.

'*Sí*,' agreed Ricardo.

Maria turned abruptly to stare at him, but he was facing away from her. She could see Nita's face, staring up at Ricardo eagerly.

'So you will be my Tio Ricardo?' demanded Nita.

'Yes,' he agreed. 'And you will come to visit us.'

'*Us*.'

All she had to do was say no. *Scream* it.

She had a headache by suppertime. Emilio was talking over dinner about the song he and Maria would be practising in the music room the next morning and she wanted to scream that she didn't want to practise. She wanted to tell them all that she was leaving, going somewhere to visit. Anywhere!

'May I listen to your practice?' asked Ricardo. He was asking Emilio. Not her!

'No!' snapped Maria.

He smiled at her across the table. 'Was that a Spanish no or an English one?'

'In any language,' she said grimly. 'In every language.' She pushed her chair back and she was standing.

'Maria!' warned her mother.

'Stop it!' Maria snapped at Ricardo, holding his eyes with hers. The table was between them but he would quietly win his way into every part of her life until she had nowhere to hide. The headache was crawling everywhere in her. Along her back and her shoulders and her hands clenching so that it was almost a scream. 'Stop manipulating me!'

'Here she goes!' murmured Emilio.

Maria realised that she was breathing as if there were no air. Glaring at Ricardo and words pressing against her throat to be screamed. He stood and came around the table, past all of them. Nothing on his face at all.

'*Con permiso*,' he murmured to the rest of them, but he did not look for their permission. He took her arm and led her out of the dining-room with him and he pushed her into Miguel's study. She heard the door slam in the same instant that he released her arm.

She swung around. His hand was still on the doorknob. He had brought her in here to stop her shouting whatever it was that she'd been about to scream in front of them all. No one had stopped him. He was the man they thought she was to marry. Not one of them was surprised if she was angry and he pulled her away to fight privately. She'd argued with Miguel often enough, and with her father when he was alive. They all knew she had a hot temper and they thought it was a lovers' quarrel.

Lovers.

'I don't want a husband.'

He inclined his head. 'Nor was I looking for a wife.'

'Then why won't you go away?' she begged.

'Come here, Maria.'

Her fingers went to her right ear and she felt the light delicacy of the jade earring there. The silence stretched. He was waiting.

She curled her fingers in on themselves. 'Why?'

He didn't answer. She swallowed and realised as she moved that she'd made no decision to put her foot forward. As if he were a magnet and she had no choice. She didn't understand why his words had power over her. She didn't want to be helpless when he looked at her. She didn't want to come when he asked. It seemed a long way across the two metres of dark carpet that cushioned the floor of Miguel's study. She stopped half a metre away from him and she would not let herself drop her eyes from his.

'Miguel thinks I need a man strong enough to bend me to his will. He's wrong.'

'Do I frighten you that much, *querida*?'

*Querida.* A lover's endearment. He'd never used it before. He stepped closer and she felt the sensations crawl along her flesh as he lifted his hands to slip them into her hair.

'Does this make you uneasy?' he murmured as his fingers threaded into her hair.

Her body trembled with the tension. The headache had shifted into muscles clenched everywhere inside her. Sensation everywhere, and she stared as his lips parted slightly and he was staring down into her eyes to read every thought that flickered there.

'Why don't you pull away?' His thumbs caressed her temples. 'Why, Maria? If you don't want this, stamp your dancer's foot and lift your head high...'

His palms tightened on her and she felt her head go back, her lips parted and his mouth so close now. She swallowed and his gaze flickered down to follow the motion along the exposed length of her throat. His thumbs slid down to possess the angle of her jaw and she felt her lips part as if it was an invitation for his kiss.

'Why not?' he asked softly. 'Why don't you leave me alone in this room? Storm past me as you did that night on Señor Descanso's balcony and leave me alone and aching for you.'

A shudder went through her. 'You'd stop me,' she whispered, mesmerised by his eyes.

'Not if you wanted to leave.'

She pulled her lip between her teeth.

'Go,' he said softly. 'Pull away now.'

She put her hands against his chest to push him away. He was wearing a raw silk suit jacket. Her hands came up inside the jacket... resting on the heat of his chest so that she could feel his heartbeat.

'Don't you understand what's happening?' he asked gently.

The heat through the fabric of his shirt was burning her hands. 'I want you to—to go.'

'No, Maria. You want me to make love to you.'

She shivered. 'I——'

He bent down and covered her lips with his. 'Like this,' he said against her mouth. He brushed his mouth across her lips with a light caress that settled against the side of her throat under her ear. 'And like this,' he murmured, pressing the warmth of his mouth against her throat. His hands were still in her hair and she gave herself up to their care.

Floating. The light caress of his mouth on her throat. His fingers massaging her scalp with a rhythm that made her lose track of what she saw until she felt her lashes brush her cheeks and he took the weight of her head and brought his mouth slowly back to hers.

'And like this,' he whispered against her lips, teasing them further apart with his mouth and stroking the wild pulse of her inner lips with his tongue.

His heart slamming against her hands. She was suspended between her hands against his chest and his fingers cradling her head gently, her hair spilling down her back and around her shoulders as he seduced her mouth with lips and tongue that advanced and retreated until she was dizzy with the beat of her heart in her veins.

He pulled a breathless moan from her throat when he took his mouth away. She tried to open her eyes. His heart beating hot under her palms and she stared up at him through heavy lids. His face was drawn with deep lines and the deep fire in his eyes.

'This is what your restlessness is rooted in.' He caressed the long length of her throat with one hand that he freed from her hair. 'Only this . . . the fire in your blood . . . Don't tell me again to leave you while that fire burns.'

His hands slid out of her hair and through it. 'Your eyes tell me the truth,' he whispered as his hands slid down along the length of her bare arms. She was wearing a green dress that left her shoulders and arms bare. She trembled as he drew his fingertips slowly back up the length of her arms and paused with his fingers lightly on her naked shoulders.

'You knew that I would be seated across from you all through dinner. Didn't you?'

'Yes,' she admitted. Her lips were still parted as if she could not close them.

'And you chose this dress to wear?'

'It was . . .' her body trembled and he stroked the inner curve of her shoulders lightly ' . . . the only thing that went with the earrings.'

His smile came slowly, as if it was an echo of the way his hands were stroking her shoulders. She could feel the sensations running ahead of his fingers so that she held her breath when he stopped and her eyes closed when his gaze was drawn to watch his own hands caressing her flesh. She breathed a sound and it was his name and she was frightened by the lost note in her own voice.

He stroked across the exposed white of her flesh above her bodice. The shudder possessed her body after his touch was gone. 'And,' he said quietly, 'you leaped up shouting at me at the table not because you were angry... but because you could not sit still any longer with me watching and you wanting——'

'No!' She felt the air flooding into her lungs, her breast heaving. She felt his hands still on her. Her eyes flew open and he was staring down at her and her breathing couldn't seem to steady as if she could not stop the motion that held his eyes on the movement of her breasts under the green satin of the dress.

'Oh, yes, *querida.*' There was no smile in his eyes when they returned to hers. 'Lie to yourself as long as you need to, but don't scream in front of your family that you will not marry me and you want me to go away when it is your own needs you are trying to escape.'

His face had changed, the mood in him changed. He stepped back, dropping his hands from her.

'I don't know what I was going to say out there,' she whispered.

He nodded, as if he believed that. 'Next time, say it to me.'

She swallowed and asked, 'Are you in love with Señora Jenan de Corsica?' She stepped back from him too, frightened that she had asked that question. Asking meant that the answer mattered. 'In Mérida they say that—that you wanted her for yourself.'

He said nothing and the wave of nausea that swept through her was pain because nothing in his face denied it.

'Would you care, Maria, if I loved her?'

She felt her fingers clench. 'No.'

'Then there's no point in my answering.'

# CHAPTER EIGHT

MARIA stood at her bedroom window and stared out over the ocean. Moonlight streaking through the low swell. She opened the window further and leaned out... stopped breathing and she could hear the sound of the surf on the sand.

The air moved against her skin. She shivered and wrapped her arms around herself. The silk of her nightgown slipped over her flesh as she moved. The caress of silk on her skin...breathless heartbeat and only the sound of harsh breathing... *his* breathing, and she'd woken wild and panicked and it was Ricardo's touch on her flesh through silk in the dream. But only her own body restless and tangled in the bedding when she woke. Alone.

She couldn't sleep with this tension. It was the headache. A summer sort of headache that went with heat and humidity. Ricardo said it was never like that where his family lived in Ecuador and she'd wondered if he meant them to live there and had screamed deep inside because it was *not going to happen*.

In the morning she would wear something much less feminine than that green satin dress. No earrings, not the gold studs and certainly not the jade pendants. Jeans, although her mother always frowned to see her in jeans. And she would tell him. Somehow she would make him believe her this time. No marriage. No seduction.

Ricardo liked her in jeans. He would kiss her. That was all he had to do to make nonsense of her attempt

130

to reject him. He needed only to stroke her skin so lightly that she felt like screaming, and the lethargy made her bones melt and she needed his mouth on hers or she would die of the hunger.

She turned from the window to look at her bedclothes tumbled across the bed in moonlight. She couldn't sleep in the place where that dream had seduced her. She would go to the music room. She would close the door and turn on the tape player. The room was soundproofed, had been constructed especially so that it could be used as a recording studio. Her first album had been recorded there and Miguel talked about opening it up for other artists to record in. He'd been talking to Señor Descanso and he thought they could make some arrangement together. That was what Ana wanted, for Miguel to be in business in a way that would keep him home. Miguel had said tonight at dinner that if Maria and Ricardo decided that she would perform less after her marriage, he would...

*Maldición*! Not the music room! Ricardo's name and his words echoing in her ears and the kiss he'd given her earlier in Miguel's office while her family sat at the dinner-table and probably said it was a good thing Maria's *novio* was not a weak man because they all knew Maria needed a strong hand.

She pulled off the gown and threw it on to the bed. She yanked open a drawer and reached for the black bathing suit but it was gone. The maid must have taken it to wash. Her hand settled on the bikini. She wore it sometimes when she went swimming alone. She loved the feel of the water slipping along her flesh.

Night-time. Moonlight outside.

She put it on. She couldn't find her towelling robe. It didn't matter. The wind was light and the water would be warm. She slipped on sandals and picked up a big towel from her bathroom. Then she escaped the restless silence of the house.

She saw the moon high up in the sky when she got outside. She hadn't looked at her watch or at the clock when she came out. Just the water outside and the night. The moon. She kicked off her sandals when she reached the sand. She could feel the grains of sand flying under her feet as she ran to the edge of the water. She ran straight in until the ocean was around her hips. She spread her hands out flat and her fingers touched the water as the slow swell rose up...then the water fell away from her as the long wave went back out to sea. She stood there motionless, staring out to sea with the water moving around her. She could see the cabin cruiser lying at anchor, its shape rising and falling with each breath the water drew.

She turned to look back at the house, a black shadow against the sky. Moonlight all around her and she stared at the black shape rising up. She stared until she could see the places where the windows were. Her window, and now that her eyes had adjusted she could see it standing wide open. On the floor above there were windows standing open too. Was Ricardo standing at the second window from the far end? Was he staring down and seeing her as a shape in the moonlight?

The water swept up and touched her waist and she shivered, although it was warm. Tomorrow she would talk to him. She would tell him that if he went away now...if he came to her in Mexico City...then she would be his lover. That was what he had wanted from the beginning. Perhaps in the end she would be like the Maya for him. When he had penetrated her secrets he would be content to turn his back and leave her.

How long would it last? Months? Perhaps only weeks after his victory. She clenched her hands and the water slipped away through her fingers. Easier if it were soon over. Not a marriage. Not his ring on her hand and nothing for her because all else was gone. If he married her he would take everything from her. Her music and the dance. He would take her far away from her home when he put that ring on her finger... and all because she had not given him the passion he had seen in her on stage. If she would be his lover outside marriage... then surely he would let her free?

She stared at the black that was the house until she saw the shape of a man coming down from the blackness. She'd called him. He was halfway down the slope that came to the beach. Walking straight towards her, and he was wearing the clothes he had worn when he'd caressed her shoulders and kissed her lips and told her that he knew the screaming was from the heavy hard pulse that twisted in her veins. Did he know that the throbbing came when he was near? Did he know that when he walked into a room she felt the restlessness and the wildness and she wanted the freedom of the stage and the dance?

He stopped at the water's edge.

'I won't marry you!' she called out. 'You told me to tell you, not to scream it at my family. So I'm telling you now. There will be no wedding.'

He was standing six or seven metres away from her. The moon did not show her his face, only his shape. His hands were at his sides loosely, not clenched with any tension.

'You shout no with the water between us... like the barrier between you and an audience. Do you think I won't come into the water?'

She tipped her head back and her hair swept down almost to her waist. 'If you send me roses in Mexico City—then I'll come to you.'

'You'll be my lover?'

'Yes.' Her fingers tightened on her own flesh under the water.

He bent down and began to take off his shoes.

'What are you doing?' she whispered.

If he heard her, he did not answer. He began to undo the buttons of his shirt. She swept the water aside with her hands. He stripped off his shirt and in moonlight she saw the naked breadth of his chest and the soft mat of curls she'd felt under her palms when she rested her hands against him. The thick pelt of hair stretched down towards his belt.

She backed up, the water almost to her breasts now. His hand went to his waist. She turned and dived into the water, pulling hard with her arms and kicking with her legs so that the water was fury around her and she would reach the cabin cruiser before he could get into the water. His hand at his belt and his muscles would ripple and catch the light and he would be naked . . . long legs and there would be dark hair on his legs . . . against her legs she would feel the soft abrasion of that hair.

She was breathless when she reached for the boarding ladder to the cruiser. The cruiser lifted up on the swell and she missed her grip, swam away and back and caught it the second time.

She reached her other hand up and she was hanging in the water from the ladder by both hands when his hand slipped around her waist and pulled her against him. She twisted and lost her grip on the ladder. There was no strength to her movement in the water, only enough to slide her body in his arms so that her back fitted against his chest intimately.

His hand clasped the ladder. He held her tightly against him, his arm across her waist. She kicked and again the protest only brought her into more intimate contact.

'You'll hide from me in Mexico City.' His voice was close to her ear.

'No...'

'Turn around,' he demanded. 'Turn in my arms and kiss me now and then tell me you want me to go.' He drew his arm away from her, his fingers sliding along the wet flesh of her midriff as he released her. She was floating, treading water, staring at the shape of him.

'Be still a moment before you run.' His voice was so quiet it should not have carried across the water between them.

'What use is there for me to run?' She swept her hands to regain her stability. 'You're stronger. You'll swim after me and catch me.'

'Have I ever held you when you wanted to be free?'

She bit her lip. 'In your jeep. When we were driving out of Mérida.'

'To keep you from leaping from a moving car.' His voice was so quiet, but she could hear a tension in it. 'You could have called the policeman we passed.'

'Tonight you dragged me into Miguel's office.'

'Dragged?'

She felt the heat crawling across her flesh. His hand on her arm and she'd walked with him and when he'd moved to kiss her later in that office her heart had gone wild because she'd wanted...

'Come here, Maria.'

She smoothed her hands away from her, swimming silently in three long strokes without breaking water. He was only a metre away now.

'Closer,' he said. 'It has to be your choice, Maria. There can be no question afterwards.'

'Afterwards?' Her voice was below a whisper. 'I'm not...'

'You waited for me...you wanted me to come down here.'

She could hear her own breathing.

'Maria, you stood in the moonlight and you saw me watching you from the window of the bedroom where I was supposed to be sleeping. Did you think I was sleeping?'

'I dreamed...' Her voice was thin like the broken ripple of moonlight when the wind caught it on a wave.

'Come,' he urged softly. 'Come and show me what you dreamed.'

Had she taken a stroke to bring herself to him? Or was it the whim of the ocean pulling her on the tide?

'Closer,' he whispered and he reached out his hand. She gave him hers and he drew her closer so that their hands were all that held them together.

'What are you wearing?' she whispered.

'Bathing trunks.'

She closed her eyes and tried to breathe.

'I promise you that you are safe.'

She dragged in air and the water was all around her and hardly any clothes between them. The man from her dreams was floating so close and his hand was tangled in hers. 'I haven't been safe since I saw you watching me from that table at La Casa del Viento. And I'm scared.'

He tugged on her hand. She reached out her free hand to stop herself slipping into his body. His shoulder was hard and warm under her grip.

'Do you want to run, Maria?'

'Yes . . . I don't know.'

'Not quite yet?' His voice was husky. 'Perhaps a kiss first?'

His lips on hers, and the water would hold her when she lost the strength to stay on her feet. 'Yes,' she breathed. 'Just . . . one.'

She wasn't ready for it. It had been in her dream and pulsing on her mouth only hours ago. But when he drew her closer she came against the hard nakedness of his chest and she could feel him all around her. His arm holding her against him and the naked breadth of his shoulders and the tight twists of the dark curls on his chest . . . naked legs brushing against hers underwater.

'Ricardo . . . I—please!'

'Hush,' he whispered. His mouth found hers and he promised, 'I promise you that if you have to run away...' his arm relaxed and she floated away until his hand at her back stopped her ' . . . I'll let you free.'

She reached up and when his mouth came on to hers she tangled her fingers in his hair, and it was the wildness and the dance, and when he pressed against her mouth with the heat of his tongue she let him in and there was nothing but the caress of the water and his mouth on her and his arm holding her against him and legs sliding gently on hers as the water moved.

When he dragged his mouth away from hers she made a sound that must have been a whimper deep in her throat.

'*Dios*! *Maria . . . querida*!'

She trembled deep inside. Her arms were wrapped around his shoulders, fingers tangled in his hair and her body floating and held against his by the tension of her own arms. She didn't know he had released her until she felt his hand move over the naked flesh of her back.

'Ricardo...I...'

'Do you want me to stop?' His voice was broken and husky. His hand caressed the sensitive flesh at her side, the long indentation of her spine. His fingers stopped at the band of her bikini-top and in her mind was the sensation that had been in her dream. 'Do you?' he demanded.

'Yes,' she whispered. 'Stop.'

His hand flattened against the skin on her back, bringing her for one second close against him. 'You have to let go too,' he said.

She realised that her arms still held him close. Circled around his neck. Close against him. She stared at his throat and in moonlight saw him swallow.

'Maria, I need words. I need to know that you want the same thing I do.'

Her heart was making breathing impossible. 'We can't—we can't make love in the water. Floating in the water.' Surely her heart couldn't beat like that and still function?

'I want to touch your breasts, Maria.' He must have heard her shaken gasp. 'Yes,' he murmured. 'I want to hear that sound in your throat...that breath that isn't quite a moan...I want to hear if you make that sound when I take your breast into my mouth and love you.'

She pushed herself away from him and floated free only a hand's reach from him. 'I don't know what to do,' she whispered. 'I'm...don't know how...if I can——'

'Tell me what you dreamed.'

'No.' He was so close. He reached out his hand and she took it. 'I can't tell you,' she said.

'Yes, you can.' He pulled her close and she was floating against him and his mouth was on hers and they were sinking into the water and he held her close in both arms and she held on tight and forgot to breathe so that it did not matter that the water was everywhere.

He brought her to the surface. The moon made his hair look blacker than black. He let her go except for one hand and he reached and placed his other hand over fabric that covered her breast. She shuddered and he pulled her and they were swimming or he was swimming and she was floating the way she did with Nita when they played in the water.

'Where? Ricardo?'

He stopped when the rocks were all around them. She stood and the water was just below her breasts and he stood in front of her and took her face in his hands and kissed her so deeply and tenderly that she melted into him.

'Did I kiss you like this in the dream?' His voice was trembling and she realised how close their bodies were. His strength pressed against her and his hand at her waist held her against him. She stiffened and he let her free, but he asked, 'Are you sure you want to go?' He touched her breast again. The lightest brush of his fingers over the fabric of her bikini-top.

'Not just yet?' he suggested.

'Silk,' she breathed. 'There was silk . . . in my dream.'

'Your skin.' He touched the smooth curve of her shoulder. 'Are you going to run?'

'Not...not yet.' She could feel the panic crawling along her veins with the other sensations. Soon she would run.

'Perhaps one more kiss?'

'Yes.' In his arms she knew that her breasts would be crushed against him again and the aching would swell her with need.

But he held her away from him as he bent down to take her lips. The movement of her body in his arms did not bring her close and the aching pressure in her breasts was worse. 'Please,' she whispered, and he swept her up so suddenly that she was dizzy, staring up into his face with moonlight showing it hard and frowning as he walked with her through the water and lowered her on to the sand.

He was leaning over her, his hand stroking the naked flesh of her arm. Moonlight on her and words on his lips telling her how beautiful she was in the loving light of the moon. Spanish words and English ones all mixed together and the trembling everywhere and his hand cupping her breast through the fabric and his thumb touching the naked flesh above. The shudder through her and no breath in her lungs.

Time to run. Past time.

He covered her lips and she opened her mouth to him with her hunger. When he broke the kiss his breathing was harsh on the night. Her hair was spread out on the sand and he stroked it.

'So beautiful,' he whispered. 'Your mouth hungry for mine.' He took her mouth again and deep in the kiss she felt his hand possess her naked breast, and it was more than she had ever dreamed. His thumb brushed rough and gentle over the peak while his hand cupped the curve and she forgot to breathe.

'*Querida*?'

He was staring down at her with his hand on her and the look on his face was something she had never seen

before. It was the moonlight and the darkness tangled
up with something shaken that echoed in his voice as he
caressed her with a lover's endearment. He bent down
and she saw his lips part as they came to her breast.
Then his mouth touched and she saw no more, only the
heat of trembling sensation that shafted from the place
where his lips possessed her to the very centre of her
woman's body.

She tried to say his name...too much...too deep,
and sensation pulsing wild in her and he left her and
there was no touch and she was crying his name but the
air was cool on her breast and his kiss gone.

'Ricardo...oh, *dios*! *Por favor*...'

His hand rested on the swollen place where he had
kissed her so shatteringly. 'Stop?' he asked. He knew
the answer, but he waited for it. She realised then that
if she asked he would take his hand away and she would
die of the needing in her.

'Not quite yet,' she whispered.

He caressed her breasts with his hands and she melted
against his touch.

'You want that?' he demanded, but when she whimpered he lay down beside her and whispered gently to
her as he took her into his arms and took her mouth
with his so that there was no need for words, only the
words of passion he whispered to her and the gentle
caress of his hands driving her mindless in his arms.

When her mouth was swollen from his kisses he left
it hungry and moved to kiss the soft swelling of her
breasts again, teasing the nipples with his tongue and
his teeth and drawing the sounds from her throat that
she could not hold back. He whispered words of love
against her and groaned when her body went restless in
his arms because it was suddenly too much sensation

and not enough and she needed . . . couldn't . . . needed to . . . love him.

His mouth against her face and his whisper in her ear. His hands caressing her back with hungry long strokes as he held her close and the tangle of hair on his chest brushed roughly over the sensitive aching of her breasts.

'Softly,' he whispered. '*Querida . . . mi amante . . .*'

The pounding of her pulse grew into a slow desperate throbbing deep inside and he held her still a long time while he stroked her back and the damp confusion of her hair and whispered to her until she could see the moon again and the shape of the man's face looking down on her.

His body was pressed against the length of hers. Her breasts were naked and pressed against him. His hand stroked so slowly down the length of her back. The long slow caress of a lover. His knee between her legs. She stiffened and her body pressed intimately against his leg and panic shot through her body.

'*Cálmate, querida.* You're safe.'

Ricardo's voice, gentle although she could feel the man's tension in his body. Ricardo was offering her the chance to run if she was coward enough to let him love her to the edge of this precipice . . . and then run from the thing that had driven her from her bed and the memory of needing and waking alone.

'I won't run,' she whispered. 'Not quite yet.'

He turned her face to his with one hand on her cheek. His mouth on hers was soft. Tender. A long kiss that held passion back. Telling her that she was safe in his arms.

'*Querido,*' she whispered. 'Ricardo . . .' Her voice trembled.

He touched her face and her swollen breasts and the trembling that was her midriff. Then slowly he drew away the last scrap of her bikini and his hand caressed the slight curve of her abdomen.

'I'm glad it's moonlight,' he whispered. 'The first time I see you . . . there should be only the moon and the night air.' His words whispered against her lips and she opened her mouth hungrily to his and when his fingers stroked the soft flesh at the inside of her thigh she felt the lightest touch into the core of her being.

He whispered to her and she could only tell him back the parts of words that could find their way past her pulsing heartbeat and the breathless wonder that was his touch on her and for a long while there was only his lips and his hands and she cried out and he spoke to her hoarsely in Spanish and told her what she told him, and when she cried out again he caressed the pulsing ache in her and she felt the wildness go loose and she was dying . . . coming apart in his arms, and he touched her still and there was a moment when she felt fear and then the fear was that his touch would stop before she . . . lost . . . cried . . . needed . . . his name on the air cried out with her voice and that was the moment when the wildness broke into pieces and she was trembling down . . . spinning and his arms around her.

Quiet . . . long quiet heartbeat and his arms holding her.

'Better?' he whispered.

His touch on her . . . the most intimate touch a woman could experience from a man's hand . . . she could feel it still pulsing inside her. She spread her hand flat on his chest. Felt the hard pulse of his heart. Closed her eyes and she could feel him hard against her. And in her body she could feel the thickening of the pulse that he had driven beyond wildness only moments ago. She put her other hand on his chest. Two hands. Two echoes of his heartbeat. He had stroked the heat of her tension and taken her past wild need to a shuddering release.

He touched her face. 'If you're going to run, *querida*, you'd better go now. There aren't many more chances.'

She slid her arms around his neck and pulled his mouth down to hers. She felt him heavy against her and when his mouth came down on hers she could feel the whole length of his body against her and she could feel his need and somewhere the old nightmare stirred but she pressed her lips against his and opened them to give him her kiss.

'You're sure?'

She tangled her hands in his hair and if she was afraid it was only an old fear that had no reason with this man. 'Ricardo...*querido*...*mi amante*...be my lover.'

'Honey,' he groaned. 'You taste like wild honey.'

He rose above her and took her face in his hand and smoothed back her tumbled hair. 'I've dreamed of you so long,' he groaned. He stroked her throat and she felt the pulse there under his hands. 'Made for my loving,' he whispered. 'When I touch you I can feel each tremble of your body. Let me show you...'

# CHAPTER NINE

WATER sliding along the length of her thigh. Husky masculine whisper against her throat. Hands...the caress so light she felt only the tingling brush of a man's hard, callused fingers as they brushed her midriff.

A murmur in her ear. 'The tide's coming in.'

She turned to find the haven of his shoulder with her face. Felt her lips press against the ridge of a muscle.

'No,' he murmured. 'I wish...but not now.'

Arms gathering her heavy sleepiness close. 'Back into the water,' the voice said. The words were like a caress as he lifted her.

Lying against his naked chest and his arms and everywhere naked and she came sharp and awake and it was no dream. His loving and she'd been throbbing in his arms and the invasion of his need into her had been an ache fulfilled...a storm of passion only dimly perceived in her fantasies.

Her nakedness was cradled in his arms. Lying against his strength as he carried her and the possession seemed total in the act of being carried. His will. His destination, and she had no weapon against this seduction because she wanted to give what he wanted to take.

He had told her that he would seduce her. She had thought the danger was to her body. Had feared a pain that her heart had told her he would never inflict on her. And now he had taught her that the passion that consumed them had nothing of the nightmare within its power...everything of her need and the deep pulsing

145

sweep of her breathing. Of life itself. Loving and giving and the need for her body to be possessed by this man. The throbbing, breathless, endless aching that only he could fill.

She hadn't known that the loving of their flesh could become only a metaphor for what happened within the heart of her being. That he would lift her and she would know that her very self was helpless in his arms. He'd taken more than her body.

'Where?' Panic in her whisper. The water sound all around and he was walking with her in darkness and the water coming up to brush her buttocks. Naked. So naked in his arms and he held her as if she were a treasure he carried...fragile and woman and all his. 'Where are you taking me?' Her voice slid clear on to the moonlit air.

'Around the rocks,' he said. He shifted her weight slightly.

'Around?' she asked. He had brought her here from the depths near the cabin cruiser. Bringing her to the place where water gave way to sand with a crescent of rocky outthrustings facing seaward. Dark with only moonlight, and a place so private that only the ocean and the white glow in the sky saw them. The place where he taught her his power over her body and her soul. And now he carried her as his trophy.

'Back to the beach,' he said. 'Where it began.'

The restless flight from her tousled bed last night. Out to the sand where she stared up at the darkness that was his window and *willed* him to come to her because she could not endure resisting the wildness inside herself even one night more. There had never been a choice. From that instant on stage when his gaze crossed the barrier between audience and performer—her fear had been real and a true warning. She had thought the danger a mere matter of touching, had feared his invasion of her fears of the old nightmare. *Tonta mujer*! Foolish woman! To believe the danger gone when she understood his need never to hurt her body. The danger was after. The danger was now. In her own need.

'*Dónde*?' she whispered hoarsely. The moon lower now, closer to the dark horizon. 'Ricardo? Please don't——'

His lips touched her words and stole them. Her eyes closed, mouth parted as he held her in his arms. His mouth took her lips as only a lover would take the woman whose soul he owned. She had no will but to give him her kiss and take the hungry penetration of his tongue into her.

'The beach?' Her words came out thick and touched by confusion when he freed her lips. Her mouth remembered the echo of another deep possession. 'The beach...the house?'

'I must return you to your bed.' Regret in his murmur, and the echo of passion. 'Alone to your bed, *querida*.'

'My bathing suit! I'm not—not dressed!'

Her words of panic did not stop him. 'Later,' he assured her. 'I'll come back to find your suit in daylight.'

He was going to carry her. Carry her naked in his arms into the house and upstairs into her bed. '*Dios*!' she whispered. 'If someone sees——!' Naked in her lover's arms.

'They won't. They're all asleep.'

'But if——' Her suit was lost somewhere in the darkness. She felt again the touch of his hands as he had released her from the last scrap of her bikini covering. Felt the breath of wind that had been the movement he'd made. He had thrown the fabric barrier aside...had come to her and she had became his and there had been no place where she did not ache for the loving that he burned to give her. But she had lost herself in him there in the secret moonlit place. Lost some part of herself that he now possessed. Something frighteningly beyond the gift of flesh and passion.

She heard the sound of water dropping away from him. She stared up into his face. His shoulders. Against her body, the sure flex of his muscular body flowed against her cradled flesh. He was carrying her back to the beach. Then to her bed. The part of her that would struggle in his arms was buried under the spell of his ownership.

'If Miguel wakes——'

'Then he wakes.' Implacable words.

He meant his possession of her to be total. She lay in his arms and she saw them both as if she were floating above somewhere. Watching Ricardo Swan as he carried his lover back into the dark silent *casa*. Up the long stairs. No one appeared to challenge his right. If Miguel came around a corner . . . he would turn away. Her brother believed that this man would soon be Maria's husband.

Ricardo walked into the room where she had tried to sleep earlier. He laid her on the narrow bed among the tumbled bedclothes and when the words came they were not a shock.

'I leave you, *mi amante*.' His mouth on hers. 'But you are mine now. Know that you are my wife.'

'No,' she whispered, but he was gone and the door quietly closed when the word came clear.

His wife . . . wife. Even now he meant to marry her! Had he possessed her in the moonlight because he could not otherwise bring her to his marriage bed?

She'd done this to herself. She had tried to preserve herself by coming to him as lover. She had intended to give him only the gypsy but he had taken everything. Fool! Had she really thought that she could play this like a part on stage? Had she believed that she could take a lover and somehow escape possession by the man?

Fool!

She threw the sheets aside and flung herself out of the narrow bed. Stood in bare feet in the middle of the bedroom that had been hers for years. The room where she had slept and dreamed and separated fantasy from the reality of her life.

The dawn was colouring the sky already. Ricardo had brought her back none too soon. Moments more and she would have been caught out there naked and——

How could she have let this happen? She'd stood there in the water and looked up at his bedroom window. Ached for him to come to her!

She had believed that once they'd become lovers he would leave her... abandon the pretence of marriage.

*My wife.*

He had trapped her. Only yesterday he hadn't denied that he loved Cathy Jenan, but he'd claimed Maria as if that didn't matter. She'd heard him deny the Latin in himself, but she'd sensed from the beginning that there was a strong vein of Spanish heritage in his heart. Not only the good, but the worst of the Spanish machismo, she realised now. God knew why, but he'd decided that he would have her. Perhaps because she had tried so hard to resist him. He didn't love her, but he would possess her.

A mystery, and he was a man fascinated by mysteries. And later... when he discovered that the excitement disappeared with the mystery, he would remember that he loved another woman. Then he would look at Maria and wish she were more like the woman he loved. A woman she could never hope to compete with. Cool and blonde and very American. *Dr* Jenan. They probably talked about Mayans, while she and Ricardo talked about odds and ends and everything else but the topic that fascinated him so.

She went into her bath and turned on the shower. Rinsed away the salt and used soap and shampoo to rinse away the loving and the memories. Ricardo Swan. It would be the biggest mistake ever. Worse than thinking she could be an American girl when she was seventeen and falling into puppy love with Wallace. Ricardo wanted her to be a wife and she'd give up everything for him and when it was over there would be nothing for her but the aching need forever.

Forever belonged to the dance. She should have remembered that. Should have kept her dreams of loving on stage where they belonged. That was where she'd made her mistake, that night in Mérida when she'd danced with him with the dance in her heart. Thinking she could reach for him as if she were on stage and it had no power to touch her life.

Maria scrubbed roughly at her body with the towel. Last night...

*Dios*! Forget last night! Forget the beach and the way he'd held her so tenderly that she'd thought her heart would break. His voice against the softness of her flesh and she'd wanted to cry because it was so much more beautiful than she'd dreamed it could be. Maybe she'd dreamed the passion, the way his touch made her melt and writhe with need at one time. Maybe she'd known a little of how that might be. She'd read books, hadn't she? She had known that sometimes it was breathlessly wonderful for a woman, and if anyone could make it like that for her it would be Ricardo. She had known that.

She didn't love him. Not the kind of 'forever' loving that Mamá and Papá had shared. This was just—if only she could forget how breathlessly beautiful she had felt...how his voice had caressed her as if she was the most precious thing in his world.

She turned on her hairdrier and switched it to its hottest setting. Promptly, the electric circuit failed.

She threw the drier down. Why was she drying her hair when her life was in ruins? *Dios*! Hadn't she known better? Crazy enough to take a lover, but to do it with her family surrounding her! They'd both be caught in this trap of a marriage and Ricardo was insane if he'd managed to tell himself he wanted it.

She clutched herself tightly, her arm hugged against her midriff.

Oh, God! That was it! Not that he'd wanted above all to possess Maria Concerta or even the gypsy. No, it was much simpler than that. The gossip was true. He loved the gringa. But she was married and in love with her husband. She was expecting her husband's child and Ricardo must feel the most terrible pain and jealousy when he saw them together. That night they danced— Juan Corsica and his wife present, and Ricardo had reached for Maria. Taken her out on the balcony and kissed her until she had screamed into his mouth. A Latin woman with long dark hair that would not remind him of short blonde curls. A woman who knew nothing of the archaeology that fascinated both him and Cathy. A woman who was...

Different. Different from the woman he loved.

She could have done something to stop it. She could have let herself have a sore ankle back at that dinner in

Mérida. She could have stayed in her bed last night instead of fleeing out into the moonlight and...and *calling* him down to her. Even later, when he'd come to her she could have said no. He'd given her chances enough.

She saw something out of the window and stopped to look down at the white expanse of sand. Ricardo. Anyone who looked out would assume he had woken early, was taking a morning walk, but he was going to find her discarded bikini. He'd told her he would and he was a man who kept his promises. *My wife!* He'd said that too, and he would make it true.

Maria went to her door and locked it. If he came to her door she would not answer.

She flung open the door of her wardrobe. The blue suitcase. Not the red—the red luggage was for La Gitana. She opened it on the bed and threw things in. She was half packed before she knew where she meant to go. Miguel was going to be furious when he realised what a fool his sister had been.

Nita would be disappointed. So would Ana.

Mamá...Mamá would be sad because she thought her daughter had finally found love. Mamá had been talking about babies and weddings and what a strong handsome man Ricardo was.

Heaven knew if she could get a flight from San José today.

Ricardo was coming up the stairs as Maria came down to find Miguel. She stopped on the third step from the bottom. He was below her, smiling up at her. She stared back at him and tried to find words.

She hadn't been prepared to find him here before she reached Miguel. She swallowed, knowing that she could not escape this, that running to Miguel and hoping to avoid this scene had been a childish fantasy.

'Maria,' he said, stepping up towards her.

She backed up on the stairs, one hand out to ward him off. 'No,' she whispered. He frowned and she saw his eyes sweep over her, then focus on her mouth.

'What did you wake up planning?' he demanded quietly.

'I haven't been asleep. I've been planning how to get away.' She saw his hand go out towards her, but he stopped the gesture himself before she backed up another step.

'One day,' he said quietly, 'you'll learn that you needn't fear me.'

'I don't want you to be here.'

'It's too late to walk away, Maria. La Gitana would understand that.'

'No,' she breathed. 'I won't be possessed by you. You've . . . you've stalked me.' His face tightened at her metaphor and she gulped but had to go on. 'You've left me no choice.'

'Last night it was you who chose.'

'Yes,' she agreed. She could not look at his eyes. Would not remember the spinning sweetness of his arms and his lips on her, his voice telling her husky words of seduction.

'And now you want to run?'

She drew in a long breath and the words came. 'I chose a lover, Ricardo. Not a husband. I never agreed to marry you. That's a trap you've made for me and I can't—I won't be—I won't be a substitute for—— If you want me to be your lover——' She gulped and that was madness because she knew now it could never be enough.

'That's impossible now,' he snapped. A muscle jumped at his jaw.

'Yes,' she agreed. 'So will you go? I never wanted a marriage! I didn't want a lover either but you— you——'

'Tempted you?' he suggested silkily.

'Yes,' she snapped. 'And I suppose you expect that I should—should *thank* you for the service of——'

'Stop it!' His hands went out to grasp her and she backed up.

'No! Don't—— You've done your bit of therapy and if you must know, it was a—a very good——' She broke off at the look of fury in his face. She hadn't expected such anger in him.

'You plan to hide yourself again? Run from what is inside you? Perhaps you can't hide, Maria. Has it occurred to you that you might have my child?' His gaze slid down over her.

She froze, then her head went up. 'I—no!'

'I was making love to my fiancée. My wife in a few weeks. There seemed no reason to take...' he reached out and cupped her chin in his palm '...precautions.' His thumb stroked her jaw. 'Perhaps you would like to reconsider?'

She shivered at the memory of her own desperate need only hours ago. The memories would be with her forever, surfacing in the dreams and the dance.

As if he could feel her thoughts, he said softly, 'You're no more able to walk away from this than I am.' He stepped back slightly and held out his arm to her. 'Come to breakfast, Maria. With me.'

'No! I won't be your wife. I won't!'

The twist of his lips did not extend to his eyes. 'One day you'll come to terms with that incredible sexuality of yours. And it will be with me.' He smiled and the smile frightened her. 'Meanwhile there's time, so long as you understand that you belong to me.'

God! Where would she end up? He was a wealthy man, a man of importance in several countries. Well educated and descended from distinguished ancestors. Latin ancestors, and although he might consider himself more *norte americano* than *latino*, she could see the Spaniard in his eyes, in the arrogance with which he had watched her when she danced and the confidence with which he had taught her body to need his passion.

She went two steps with him, then she pulled away. 'I don't want your wedding-ring,' she said clearly.

Miguel was coming out of his office. He stopped and stepped back away from them when he heard Maria's raised voice.

'No!' said Maria sharply, but her brother turned back into his office and left her alone with Ricardo.

'It's between us,' said Ricardo.

'Yes,' she agreed. She felt a muscle in her throat jerk. 'You've done that. With this fiction of our marriage you have taken my family's protection away from me.'

His eyes narrowed. 'You weren't asking for protection last night.'

'I said I would be your lover.' Her whole body was trembling, shivering deep inside. 'You said marriage and I said I wouldn't, but I told you I would be your lover. Damn you!' She gulped and muttered, 'Give me presents if you must. Jewels and that handbag. Gold and silver, and you said rubies. All right! But not a wedding-ring!'

'That's what you want? To be only my mistress?' He was standing rigidly, his hands clenched. She stared at his right hand.

'You've done all this—my brother and my mother and—*dios*! How am I to tell them that it was all—you've deliberately trapped me!' She bit her lip when his hand clenched into a tighter fist as if he really wanted to strike her.

He reached out with the hand that had been a fist and touched her shoulder. She felt her traitorous body sagging against his.

'There's nothing you need tell them,' he gritted out. 'You marry me next month. The rest we will settle between us. All this——' He shook her slightly. 'Maria, you needn't fear. This wouldn't be happening now if I hadn't had to leave you earlier. Once we are married——'

'Do you think I would marry a man like you? A man who never listens to my protests, who takes his own desires as my wishes?' She pulled back and he let her go so suddenly that she staggered.

'Your wishes?' he echoed.

'Yes! My wishes! You didn't ask me about this marriage! I don't want you! I won't have you! It's over now! Now! And if you're not leaving this house, I'm leaving!'

He blocked her motion towards Miguel's office. 'You haven't the faintest idea what you want. You're so wrapped up with your stage image that you wouldn't know where to find the woman inside if you fell over her.'

She curled her fingers in on themselves and made a smile come. The gypsy's smile. 'The stage image is what you wanted, isn't it?' she demanded silkily. 'You want the gypsy to be real, because she's least like the woman you really love.' Her breath went in and out in a rage and that was when she realised she was angry, furious and flaming because he didn't really care enough to stop her sending him away. 'Do you think of her when you make love to me?' she asked wildly. 'Do you think of Cathy?'

Something flashed over his face and she realised with a sick wave of horror that it was more than a fear. It was true. Catherine Jenan de Corsica was the woman Ricardo wanted in his arms. The wife he wanted. She felt the angry heat flare and knew that she'd wanted what she was trying to throw away: this man at her side, in her life. Wanted it and feared it.

'It's you I want,' he said. He reached for her and she backed away.

'Your voice lacks conviction, *querido*.' She made the endearment mocking and it tore at her heart. 'But if you want the fantasy of the gypsy, just...' she almost choked on her own words ' . . . just come to my concerts. I'll sing for you.'

She spun, and his hand flashed out so that instead of storming past him she came slamming into him, hard against his chest and she could feel his breathing hard and angry against her breast. 'This is ridiculous,' he muttered. 'There's only one way to discuss this with you!' His mouth bent towards her.

'No! Don't touch me!' She was free with her breath pulsing panic in her chest.

'Maria!'

'Don't ever touch me again!' She stuck her hands out with palms out. 'Stop! I—I—I'm terrified of you! I don't want you to touch me!'

He froze, then deliberately pushed his hands into his pockets. 'Then go,' he commanded. 'Get the hell away from me before I give in to temptation to shake the damned stupidity out of you!'

She gulped. What in God's name was she doing? Why was she doing this? She'd come downstairs scared and now she felt only confused. He always confused her. Away from him she sometimes had some faint idea of her own mind, but when he was near...

'Are you going?' he demanded. 'Make up your bloody mind for once and for all. Are you afraid of me? Or have you the courage to reach for what we both know you want?'

She swallowed, feeling the confusion and the terrible lack of will that slid over her whenever he was near. 'Do you...do you love her?' she asked on a whisper. 'Tell me...tell me the truth, Ricardo.'

He looked tired. 'Cathy isn't the issue between us.'

'I want to know.'

He shrugged. 'Yes, then. Once I thought I was in love with her.'

'When?'

'Last summer. Before she married Juan.' He asked drily, 'Do you want details? This makes no difference to us, Maria.'

'I want myself back,' she whispered. 'And it's my house. You're the one who should go.' She knew she could not shout, could not make him. If he reached for her she would be his. It was true and it terrified her because he'd just admitted that he'd wanted the same thing from another woman that he now claimed to want from her.

Only last summer.

'Is that what you really want?' he asked soberly. 'For me to leave?'

She nodded. She couldn't speak.

'I won't be back this time.'

She nodded again. It would be over. Inside she could feel the pain rising, but when he was gone she would learn to get past the pain. She would be herself again. Safe again.

He had both hands in his pockets again. He stepped back from her. She stared at his chest and could not look into his face. She was scared and didn't know which she feared most: that he would walk away... or would reach for her and expose the aching need in her heart. Loving when she'd known it was beyond danger to love like this... to let the passion escape the dance.

'What if you're carrying my child?' he asked.

'I won't tell you,' she said. 'I don't ever want to see you again.'

# CHAPTER TEN

LA GITANA bent her head as the music faded. As she came out of her deep curtsy the roar of the crowd throbbed through her body. This is how it will be always, she thought. I'll always be alone when the music fades.

Shouts and screaming and the roar of hands striking on hands. Mexico City applauding the gypsy with enthusiasm. Miguel was off stage grinning, his hand raised in a gesture of victory. Mamá was sitting in the chair that gave her a view of the stage and let her rest at the same time.

'*Magnífica*!' called Miguel, his voice drowned in the roar from the crowd. He waved her back for the first encore. Two encores if the crowd demanded. They had decided that in practice, and which songs they would do. The first was 'La Gitana', the first song she had ever recorded. She had sung it in Mexico and in the States, and she had sent it over the television waves in one variety show she'd appeared on. Tonight it would be broadcast on satellite television to Mexico, but she let her eyes close as she threw back her head and she *would not* let herself wonder if he could be watching. He would be in some other country by now, and why would he watch Mexico's satellite? He probably only watched educational television.

She went off stage when the song ended, but they roared for her again. She saw Miguel nod towards Emilio who was watching him from his position left-stage. Then she realised which song they were calling for.

The Lisbon love song. 'Amor de Lisbon'.

'No,' she whispered, but the music was coming. The song she'd refused to sing tonight.

She went back into the music. The haunting melody that had first caught her in the spell of the man watching. Except that he was not watching. Would never watch again. And here in this massive concert hall Miguel's intimate trick with the lighting was impossible.

Catherine Jenan de Corsica. That was the woman in his heart. He hadn't been able to deny it. But he'd wanted Maria too. *Wanted*. And she'd wanted——

He'd said she didn't know what she wanted, but in the last notes of the love song she knew that coming off stage into emptiness was what she'd won for herself. She loved Ricardo. Ached for him with an intensity she'd never known was possible. The insanity was that it was the very strength of her loving that had panicked her into turning him away from her, screaming at him in the hallway of her own home and throwing words at him until the thing that had made him pursue her was gone.

He'd wanted her from the beginning. Lust, but perhaps if she'd let his crazy proposal of marriage happen his passion might have grown into love.

Or he might have spent the years wishing she were a different woman. That was what she'd run from, that and the knowledge of how deeply he'd possessed her. She'd thought her life would return to what it had been before. That a month would bring her numbness and the ability to enjoy her family and her life as she had in the years before he walked through the barrier between performer and audience.

She had been wrong. She hadn't dreamed how much it would hurt. She hadn't realised that other lovers would haunt her so, reminding her of what she had sent away. Miguel speaking his wife's name, and Maria could hear more than affection. She could hear the mysterious thing that made a man and a woman one against the world. Emilio speaking of Señorita Descanso with his eyes unfocused as if her name brought her image too powerfully. Mamá looking sad because Maria's mother had dreamed. But, despite the fantasy of the dance, Maria herself hadn't had the courage to dream when the stage lights dimmed and the audience went home.

Miguel and Emilio crowded around her on her way to the dressing-room. Mamá was talking about flowers and Maria felt her heart stop as she entered the dressing-room because she was looking for one special flower. Ricardo's flower. The red rose he always sent.

Orchids on the dressing-table. Roses too. White and...and red! Maria pushed through the stage manager and her brothers in a rush to the dressing-table.

Red roses and white and pink. All mingled together into one bouquet.

'Who sent them?' she whispered. No one heard her. She reached out one hand for the card nestled in the flowers, but hope was gone.

Señor and Señora Descanso. Not Ricardo's thick black writing. Not Ricardo.

Mexico City. They'd talked about it often enough. About Ricardo's coming to her in Mexico City. He'd meant to pursue her there, to claim what he'd insisted her eyes promised him. He'd taken that on the beach near San José del Cabo and he'd been willing to marry her in return. But although he'd called her his lover in Spanish, he'd never said that he loved her...had never asked for her love.

He'd claimed her, and that was why she'd felt so frightened of his power over her. Because he was predator and victor and owner. He gave her passion and tenderness and patience, but when she sent him away it tore her heart apart and merely made him angry.

She showered off the heat and perspiration of the performance. She was calm again when the dressing-room door opened for those important enough to be invited backstage. Miguel and Emilio mingled through the backstage crowd, watchful for problems and ready to send them all away when they'd had their fifteen minutes of Maria. Miguel put a glass in Maria's hand and she sipped it slowly. *Agua mineral*, although the others drank champagne. She sipped and nodded and none of them wanted her to answer questions badly enough to press her when she smiled and agreed. A performance. She might be singing a song. She agreed with the dark frowning man in front of her without knowing what he'd said.

She turned away with a smile to the next person.

A beautiful blonde woman standing beside a man who had one arm around her. Juan Corsica and his wife. Maria managed a smile somehow. Catherine Jenan de Corsica. Ricardo called her Cathy. Her eyes were glowing and her pregnancy was unmistakable even in the loose silk gown she wore.

'I thought you'd left Mexico,' Maria managed to say.

Catherine grinned and a look flashed between her and her husband that made Maria ache. 'We arranged tickets to this performance when we realised we were going to be stopping over in Mexico City at the same time you were here,' explained Cathy. 'After seeing you in Mérida, I couldn't resist.'

'We wanted one more visit to Mérida,' Juan Corsica added with a courteous smile. 'Before Catalina stops travelling.' Another of those looks between the couple, and Maria knew that the Corsicas had disagreed over Cathy's travelling. Catalina, her husband called her, and perhaps she was neither so quiet nor so cool as she appeared.

Had Ricardo reason to know that?

'An enthralling performance,' said Juan, bowing to Maria.

'Thank you. Is—is Ricardo with you?' Cathy's eyes narrowed and Maria knew she should not have asked. She'd tried to make the question casual, but her voice must have given away something.

'The last I heard,' said Cathy, 'he was buried in artefacts at UCLA.'

'I thought he wasn't going back there?' said Maria faintly.

'He sent Catalina twenty thousand *pesos*,' said Juan suddenly.

Maria nodded, confused and not caring. He was back at the university. A passion for mysteries but the mystery of La Gitana was gone now and he'd forgotten her.

Cathy said, 'Juan, I don't think——'

The Peruvian shook his head. 'You're wrong, you know,' he said, touching his wife's shoulder as if in reassurance. 'Ricardo once interfered between us.' He was smiling as if the memory were pleasant, but somehow there must be something else between them that didn't show in Juan's smile and his wife's worried frown. Maria turned away. She could not bear any more of this.

The blonde woman stopped Maria with a hand on her shoulder. 'I think I should tell you about this bet. It was at that restaurant where Ricardo first heard you sing. We went there because Professor Talamtes saw you were performing and Ricardo wanted to please him.'

Maria shook her head. 'No,' she whispered. 'I don't want to hear.' *Dios*! Had it all been some terrible joke? Ricardo loving her, and it was only a wager made over drinks at La Casa del Viento?

\* \* \*

The shuffling in the lecture hall ceased as Ricardo walked into the room. He dropped a small pile of books on the desk and stepped up to the lectern. His students stared up at him expectantly.

His students, but he'd seen little of them this term. Gary had taken the lectures while Ricardo was finishing up at Mérida, and only weeks ago Ricardo had thought he might not return at all except for a few lectures to ensure that the faculty wasn't left in chaos by the head of department's sabbatical.

He spread his notes and began to talk about *haab*, the Mayan solar vague year calendar. How in heaven's name had he drifted into this? He'd known from the moment he took charge of his father's mining empire that it wasn't what he wanted for himself. His father had been an ambitious man who hated to lose. He'd made his life from ambition and the fierce desire never to give up his possessions. Ricardo's mother numbered among the possessions, and Ricardo had known from his youth that his mother was trapped in a marriage she regretted.

Mixed cultures. His mother had come from the Spanish traditions of Ecuador, his father from the wilds of northern Canada. His mother was old money and his father new ambitious power. They understood nothing of each other and Ricardo had taken the lesson of his childhood to heart, so much so that a year ago, at thirty-nine, he'd never even contemplated marriage. He'd always told himself that if he did marry, it would be someone from his chosen culture. An American or a Canadian. A woman who cared about the things he cared about. Who expected exactly the same things from a marriage that he expected.

Dr Catherine Jenan had seemed ideal. He'd seen her on television first, had been caught by her coolness and intrigued that a slender girl who looked so young could have amassed the academic credits she had. And when he had decided to ask for her to photograph the Yucatán excavation, he'd looked forward to meeting her. And yes, after he had met her he'd hoped they might become more than friends and colleagues.

His ideal woman. She shared his interest in archaeology and she came from a cool, rational culture. And when he met her he liked her open friendliness. He'd liked her.

She'd liked him too, but there hadn't been any sparks on her side. He had realised that almost at once. Still, he had pursued her, thinking liking might grow into more... until he'd realised that she was already deeply in love with another man. And when he had seen Cathy in love, he'd realised that she wasn't the cool, rational woman he'd thought her. Perhaps love did that to people: made them wildly irrational.

He'd taken a sort of pride in the marriage between Cathy and Juan. It had given both of them an aura of unmistakable happiness, and Ricardo had played a role in getting them together. But although he'd been glad to see their happiness he'd been relieved that it wasn't him. That he had retained his equilibrium. That no woman had the power to do to him what Catherine Jenan did to Juan Corsica.

'But why is it called the vague year?' asked a student in the second row.

For a moment, Ricardo wondered what the girl was talking about. He'd been talking, automatically following his notes, but it was time he got his mind on what he was doing. It was hardly fair on the students for their professor to wander around with his mind on a woman who was a thousand miles away.

A world away.

He'd never intended to watch the concert. He hadn't realised that it was to be televised until Cathy turned up in his office a week ago.

'Juan and I are flying to Mérida for the weekend,' she'd announced, flushing.

'Second honeymoon?' he'd asked, smiling when her flush deepened.

'Well——' She'd shrugged and smiled. 'We like Mérida.'

He supposed they did. It was the place where they had decided to stop tormenting each other and make their lives together. It was at Mérida's airport that Juan had come to stop his love leaving his life forever. At that airport where Cathy had looked up at Ricardo and said, 'I'm getting married.' Later there had been a church ceremony and Ricardo hadn't been there to watch, but he'd seen them together in the airport and he'd known that the real vows had been exchanged there. The commitment to each other forever.

Maria...

'Enjoy yourself,' he'd said to Cathy last week. 'The baby's due next month, isn't it?'

'Yes, and this is my last flight. Mérida and back through Mexico City. We've got tickets for La Gitana's concert there. I was going to tune in the satellite and watch her from our living-room in San Francisco, but I realised we're actually going to be flying through Mexico City the first night of her performance.'

Maria, dancing. He had felt the tight pain deep in his gut and known that it wasn't going to go away any time soon. That was when he'd pulled out his wallet. He still had a few Mexican bills there that he hadn't exchanged. As if he meant to return, but there was no reason now. The excavation at Mérida had been handed over to the university at Mérida, and as for Maria... He'd been insane to think that could work. Different cultures. Different lives.

He'd pulled out the bill and handed it to Cathy.

She'd been confused, staring at it. 'Do you want me to change it for you? I guess I could give you dollars for it. I can use it when we——'

'No. I owe it to you.'

She'd shaken her head.

'Did Professor Talamtes pay up on that bet?'

She smiled. 'Well, yes.'

'Pay him back. He was right.' He folded her hand around the bill.

'La Gitana?' Her eyes widened.

'Maria. Yes.'

'Are you——?'

'No,' he'd said abruptly. 'We're not, and we won't. But he was right, so pay him back when you see him.'

'But why?' persisted the student in the lecture hall. 'The Mayans had such accurate calculations for the movements of the solar system. Why didn't they figure out they were a quarter-day off on the solar year?'

He heard himself explaining. He'd explained it before, had always enjoyed watching students' curiosity awakened about history and the peoples who had been on the earth before concrete buildings and spaceships.

He was tired of it. Tired of everything. It all seemed colourless.

It had always been colourless, he supposed, except that he hadn't known until he saw her dancing. Until he walked with her in carnival and saw her laugh, saw her face light up with appreciation of a beautiful weave in a hanging blanket. She saw the world in colour and beauty and emotions, and standing at her side he too could see the colours and feel the beauty of it. If he'd gone to Mexico City, he would have sent her a rose. She would have seen it in her dressing-room after the performance. And then——

Then what? Pursuit again? A shudder shook him and his voice turned harsh so that the student asked no more questions. He flipped a page on his notes and made himself concentrate. What use to pursue her again? Perhaps he could trap her again, catch the mood of her dance and capture her in her own fantasy. That was all it had been. When daylight came she'd run quickly enough... had remembered soon enough all the things she did not want.

When had he become a man driven to possess the woman he lusted after? When had it become too little to have her as his lover and not enough to know she cried out his name when he was loving her? When had he become so trapped in her spell that he spent four hours calling everyone he knew until he found someone with a satellite dish capable of bringing in a Mexican broadcast for him to watch four nights ago?

La Gitana, but as he watched her he saw his Maria... the woman who had stared up at his window from the beach... the girl who had swum away from him, caught in their spell but nervous... the girl on the balcony who had responded to his kiss and then frozen with the horror of memories he'd never dreamed were trapped inside her... the lover who had held his hand walking a beach north of Mérida and laughed when he smiled. Who had looked at him over a little girl's head and made him ache to have *their* child standing between them.

At the very end of the concert, she sang the love song that had first made him believe she was his. He'd been a fool to watch her image on television, to torture himself with memories and desires that had never had a chance.

'Your term papers are due this Friday,' he reminded the students as he dismissed them. They groaned and began to break up. Some came up to the front of the lecture hall and, from their questions, his lecture must have been more coherent than his thoughts.

' . . . don't you agree?' demanded an elderly man who was taking the course to expand his horizons.

'With what?' queried Ricardo.

Across a milling crowd of heads he thought he saw something. A lush abundance of black hair. Would he spend his life in aching desperation every time he saw a girl with long, black, abundant curls? He thought of the piece of paper in his wallet, the address written down only that morning when he was on the telephone. If he went to her again, what would be different? She'd made it plain enough that, despite their physical chemistry, she found his pursuit a form of torture. It was over. Only a fool would go back.

He tried to listen to the elderly man, but the black hair moved closer and he caught a glimpse of red and it was her colour.

If he was a fool, then so be it. There seemed no choice.

It probably didn't matter what she wore, but she'd changed her clothes three times. First she put on jeans and a cotton blouse because that seemed to fit with a visit to a university. Students all wore jeans in the States, she remembered.

But she wasn't a student. And if she dressed like one he would know it was a costume. So she changed and next was a dark sheath that needed her hair up to look right. That made her look like a tailored gringa, and that might be a more suitable role but it wasn't her by any wild stretch of the imagination. Especially the tightly rolled coil of hair. Another costume, she realised as she stared at the image of the woman in the mirror.

She pulled off the sheath and yanked out hairpins.

She put on the red dress then. It was cotton, casual and loose enough so that the skirt swirled slightly when she walked. The bodice was buttoned and she left the top button open so that the gold cross she wore peeked out. Her father had given her that cross for her fifteenth birthday. She had always worn it since that day.

She brushed her hair out but it was too wild, an undisciplined riot of curls. In the end she compromised by containing its freedom with two combs that left the curls free to tumble down her back.

She frowned at her image in the mirror, but she would never manage to look either cool or blonde. She looked exotic. Her hand was shaking as she put on lipstick. She didn't add any other make-up. She wasn't going on stage and her colouring didn't need make-up.

She took a taxi to the university from the hotel. She knew that her aunt would be hurt if she realised Maria had come to Los Angeles without visiting her. Later perhaps. She could not bear questions now. She had a collection of voices in the turmoil of her mind already and one more would be more than she could bear.

Cathy, saying, 'I felt safe enough betting twenty thousand *pesos* that he wouldn't fall under the beautiful gypsy's spell. Less than ten dollars American, and Ricardo was always so cool.'

He hadn't been cool with her.

Ricardo, telling her, 'If you want my thoughts and feelings, you know well enough how to prod them to the surface,' his voice holding anger subdued.

Miguel, saying, 'He won't come back now. You'll have to go to him now,' and herself denying that she would ever go begging to a man.

Juan Corsica saying, 'I always said I hoped one day——'

No! Crazy to replay that comment. Juan's guess, and how could he know what might be in Ricardo's heart?

She couldn't find the lecture hall.

'Wednesdays he lectures at two when he's on campus,' Cathy had confided. She'd given directions to the lecture hall, but Maria must have taken a wrong turn somewhere. Then she saw the number on a closed door, and as she pulled it open she heard the voice that made her heart stop. His voice. She felt exposed as she came into the lecture hall. She was certain that he would look up and see her, catch her exposed in the doorway, perhaps even tell her harshly that she didn't belong in this lecture, that she wasn't a student.

What if he looked at her with only irritation in his dark eyes? Or hatred.

She sat in a seat on the aisle, beside a young man with red hair that was longer than Maria's. Ricardo was talking about the Mayan calendar. She looked around her and the students were all caught in his spell. A handsome man, tall and dark and commanding, standing at that lectern and weaving a spell as he told of the mysterious science of a proud race.

He'd never really talked to her about this sort of thing except that day at the archaeological site. Probably he had no idea she would be interested. Their time together had always been so filled with tension and confusion and she'd been afraid... afraid of seeming stupid if she asked the wrong questions. She knew so little of this world that fascinated him.

Somewhere in the front rows a hand went up. Ricardo stood with one hand in his pocket while he listened to a question that even Maria thought wasn't very perceptive. He answered it seriously and a small discussion between the man at the lectern and a few of the students ensued. Then he brought their attention firmly back to the material he was presenting and Maria thought that the students who had asked the questions were firmly caught in his spell now if they hadn't been before.

She made herself watch him with the critical eye of a professional performer, but there were no weaknesses to catch. He had the charisma of a man with total confidence in himself. He stood there and he enthralled them with the past and when the students asked questions he seemed pleased by their curiosity. He was a natural teacher. He would be a wonderful father. He would lead his children without crushing them. Just as he had led her into passion without stirring the old terror by forcing her.

She hugged herself and only realised how tightly her arms were wrapped around her midriff when the boy with the long hair gave her a curious glance.

'You OK?' he asked.

She nodded. She was terrified. Ricardo would be finished in a minute. She didn't know how long the lecture lasted, but she could sense his words moving to a completion. They'd all get up and what would Ricardo do? Turn and leave through that door behind the lectern? Would she be able to push through the students in time to get to him before he disappeared into the endless corridors of this building?

If she did, if she reached him, what would she find in his eyes? Would he send her away? As she had sent him out of her life? Would he want her now? And if he did, what would be in his heart?

Shivering in the lecture hall with his voice talking about term papers, she admitted her cowardice to herself. She'd been running for years. She'd run when Wallace had turned her adolescent dreams into a nightmare. She could have stayed, could have gone on with her musical training and pretended that nothing had happened ... but she'd run. And she'd hidden herself behind her brothers, avoiding any other contact with men on an individual basis. Afraid to face up to her sexuality even though she knew well enough that not all men were like Wallace ... that many women had relationships of love and passion.

But she'd been afraid. Uneasy when Ricardo slipped through her barriers. Terrified as she realised that her greatest danger was from inside. She was Ricardo Swan's prey, and somewhere in the dance of his seduction she had realised the essential truth that was most frightening of all. She had become his prey because she consented to be. The power he had over her...her inability to escape him came from within herself. He was a danger to her because she could not escape his touch on her heart. Miguel had been enough to discourage all the other men, but she hadn't cared about any of them. Hadn't loved them.

She was in love with Ricardo.

Perhaps she'd been in love with him from that first meeting of eyes in the dimmed lighting of La Casa del Viento. She supposed it was only to be expected that she'd run from that truth as she'd run from everything from the night Wallace had taught her that dreams didn't always translate into reality. She'd learned that lesson well, had kept the dreaming on stage in all the years since.

She had been too much of a coward to try for the dream Ricardo offered her. Marriage to a man who was more than her dreams. It would have been a terrible risk. Marrying a man who made sensuality seem a paradise of anticipation instead of a thing to be feared. But he was the same man who had never shown her a single crack in his own mask.

Or had he? 'If you want my thoughts and feelings, you know well enough how to prod them to the surface...'

He'd been furious the last time she saw him. Anger. What might have been concealed under the anger? Cool, Cathy said, but he hadn't been cool with Maria.

She was on her feet with the others. Standing but frozen. She made herself move towards the front of the hall. There were stairs down through the seats and she could see his head as she moved closer. Then he turned and looked straight at her, then away.

Had he seen her?

She bit her lip hard and made herself go on. A gamble, and she was a woman who had learned not to take chances with men. But the only alternative was to go back to a life without the man she loved. That seemed no choice at all.

Then she lost sight of him because she was at the bottom of the stairs and there were so many tall young men in this crowd of students. When she pushed past a tall dark man who might have been Ricardo if she hadn't seen his hawkish face, the stranger murmured something to her.

She shook her head and pushed on. She wasn't sure what he'd said. Something about, had she been in this class all along. Probably they would throw her out when they realised she didn't belong. A woman in front of her turned hurriedly and collided with Maria. 'Sorry,' she breathed, and dodged around.

Ricardo was standing directly in front of Maria now. His head was turned away from her, one hand still casually in his pocket and the other holding a sheaf of notes that he must have been working from during the lecture. If he'd been reading from notes it certainly hadn't shown. The notes would be reminders, but he'd spoken spontaneously, with the eloquence of a man confident of his own knowledge and his audience's interest.

He nodded and turned away from the young man he'd been talking to. Someone touched his arm and he said something. Then everything went still and quiet.

His eyes locked on hers.

He didn't say anything, not a word. Just stood there and stared at her and she tried to tell herself that he wanted her here, in front of him and only a hand's reach away. But she stared into his eyes and she saw emotion but could not tell what it was. Anger? Impatience? She swallowed and swallowed again and cast desperately in her mind for the words she'd practised.

Hello, Ricardo. *Buenas tardes*, mi amante...

Someone was talking. The sounds came back in on Maria suddenly and she realised that the woman in blue was repeating a question. Something about computer models and telescopes confirming the Mayan measurements.

Ricardo stepped towards Maria. No words, but from the look in his eyes she thought that he meant to send her away. She had no place here. He'd once asked if she wanted to visit him in Los Angeles, but he'd never repeated that offer. Even during the fiction of their upcoming marriage there had been no mention of his bringing her up to the States. No mention of where they would live, and she knew now, looking into his eyes, that he'd never meant the marriage to happen. That night when he'd made love to her... what he'd said when he laid her naked in her own bed had been a moment of madness, the spell of their loving still on him, and he'd never meant her to be anything more than his Mexican lover.

She stepped back.

He stopped.

She froze.

'Excuse me,' he said to the blue woman. 'I have an appointment.'

He stepped towards Maria and took her arm in the way a man possessed a woman's body to guide her in walking. He was taking her with him. Going somewhere a little more private before he told her she wasn't welcome. Because he had been her lover and perhaps he thought he owed her privacy for this rejection.

She trembled as they walked together. He hadn't said even her name. She heard someone whisper, 'There you are, Molly! I told you a hunk like that had to be taken already.'

He opened a door and gestured her to go through ahead of him. On the other side the corridor was quieter than the lecture hall had been. He picked up a pile of books as they went out and she found his touch gone from her arm. Walking side by side and no words. Every step made it more impossible to find words.

Where are we going?

He stopped at a doorway that led off the corridor. He had keys in his hand and he opened the door. He held it for her. 'My office,' he said, as though he thought she was envisaging a torture chamber. Heaven knew, he might read that in her eyes.

She gulped and preceded him into the room.

# CHAPTER ELEVEN

'WHAT does this costume represent?' Ricardo's voice had the cool sound of indifference.

She had walked to his window to stand staring down at a courtyard full of milling students. 'Costume?' she asked, turning back to look at him.

He was closing the door to the office. There was nothing in his expression to suggest that he hoped this might turn into a sensual interlude. 'I've seen you many times in costume. Your American tourist costume at carnival.' He dropped his keys into his pocket. 'Maria at home dressed in a bathing suit and not planning to have guests... Maria the seductress in a bikini by moonlight.'

She bit her lip. 'You think this is another costume?'

He dropped the books on to his desk. 'Of course.' He studied her and said musingly, 'You're not La Gitana today, or the water nymph who stood costumed in a suggestive bikini to draw me down to the beach. But——'

'It's not a costume.' Her hands tangled in the folds of the red skirt and she remembered how she had stood in front of the mirror and rejected the cool look with hair up, the student blue-jeans costume. 'It's just Maria,' she whispered. Where had her determination gone? She'd vowed she wouldn't let his eyes turn her brain to confusion, but already her voice was rising and nothing would be different.

'Have you come to tell me you're going to have my child?'

She gasped and her hands gripped the sill of the window behind her. 'Is that what you thought when you saw me in the lecture hall?'

'Yes.' Anger in his eyes.

Her gaze locked on his face. 'What will you do if I say there is a baby, Ricardo?'

'Marry you.'

She shivered. Looking in his eyes, she understood now why she had been afraid of the marriage he had seemed so determined to bring about. Not only did he not love her, but he did not want to love her.

'You never asked me to marry you,' she whispered. 'You announced it to my family, but you never asked me.'

'Are you pregnant?'

She shook her head mutely, knowing what would come next. Then why are you here, Maria?

'I enjoyed your performance Saturday night.' He moved something on his desk. She couldn't see what it was.

'You weren't there at the concert. I know you weren't.'

He looked up and she saw that he was almost smiling. 'Would you have known in that mob?'

She gulped and nodded. Even if he had not sent her red roses, she would have *felt* him near.

'I saw you on television.'

'Oh.' She licked her lips and wondered what on earth she had thought would happen when she faced him again. Had she thought he would reach for her and she would come into his arms this time without hesitation?

'Do you have plans for dinner, Maria?'

'I—no.' An empty hotel room. In two days she had to fly back to Mexico, but she might as well go tomorrow.

'Will you have dinner with me?'

She parted her lips but the words wouldn't come and in the end she simply nodded.

'At my place.'

'Yes,' she agreed. 'I—anywhere.'

'I have a place on the beach,' he said deliberately.

'All right.'

He gave her an odd look, but said nothing.

They walked out to his car through long corridors where he was stopped twice, both times by other faculty members. He introduced her to one, a grizzled man with a long moustache. He said her name and she wanted him to say something more. To tell her what he thought she would be to him.

My friend . . . my lover . . . the woman I . . .

'Maria,' he said. 'Maria Concerta.'

The grizzled man spoke to her in Spanish. Then they were at the car and driving and she tried to relax.

'Where are you staying?' he asked. 'Does your aunt still live here?'

She tangled her fingers in her handbag. 'Yes, but I'm at a hotel.'

'Is your family with you?'

She shook her head. He glanced at her and she realised he hadn't seen. 'I'm alone,' she said. Alone except for Ricardo, and they were speaking so formally that they did not need a chaperon to guarantee coolness between them.

He drove north of the city and finally turned into a long winding drive that led to the sea. When he stopped the car he had both hands on the wheel for a long time before he spoke.

'Do you want to go back to the city?'

Her heart pounded against her ribcage. 'Why?'

'A beach house.' He turned his head, his hands still gripping the wheel. 'I suspect the thought of a California beach house—I don't want to stir old nightmares.'

She glanced at the house and suddenly his hesitation over asking her here took on a new meaning.

'We'll go into town,' he said. His hands seemed to grip the wheel tighter.

'No.' She touched his arm but felt the muscle tense as if in rejection. 'Maybe I will always be a bit nervous of strange men, especially big men. But you——' She swallowed and wasn't sure she had the courage to say the words. 'But you could never make me afraid in that way. I know you would never hurt me.' She felt the heat in her face as she admitted, 'When I think of . . . of . . .' She closed her eyes tightly and got the words out. 'When I think of being with a man now it's you I think of, not Wallace. It's . . . you and the moonlight and being on the beach and . . .' She couldn't say any more. She'd come to tell him everything in her heart, but her courage could only take her so far when she didn't know how much he wanted to hear.

He took his hand away from the wheel and placed it gently against her cheek. 'Thank you, Maria,' he whispered. 'That couldn't have been easy to say.'

'No,' she agreed. 'But I—I wanted to say it.'

'Shall we go in, then?'

The uncomfortable quality in the tension was gone. She went with him into the beach house and somehow ended up in his kitchen chopping onions and crying from the fumes while he put two steaks into a frying-pan. Then she washed the onion tears out of her eyes and moved through his rooms touching the leather of the sofa and the smooth varnished wood of his antique desk.

'I can tell this is your place,' she said when she came to the window.

'How's that?' He was watching her.

She turned to face him, leaning back against the varnished desk. 'Latin and *norte americano* blended together.' He was watching her with nothing more than curiosity in his eyes, but as she leaned back against the desk she saw it all change and he was the man on the other side of the barrier—but, unlike the others, he had the power to cross any barrier that contained her heart.

'Are you in love with Cathy?' she asked. 'You told me once that you'd thought of... that you'd been interested in her. Are you still in love with her?'

He didn't move, but she saw his eyes go quiet and knew he was containing his reaction inside the safety of his mask. He said she wore costumes, but watching him she understood how he had recognised the part of her that played parts.

'Does it matter?' he asked.

She must hold courage close, not run from truth if there was to be any hope. 'I think I could live with anything else,' she whispered. 'But not that. Not... your wishing I were another woman.'

He had something in his hand. A glass, she thought. She couldn't see it clearly because her eyes were locked on his face, needing to read what was there. He set whatever it was down and stepped closer to her. He came halfway across the carpeted distance that separated them.

'Cathy—I thought she was what I wanted.'

'And was she?'

'No.' He moved closer. If she reached out now she could touch him. She was leaning back against the desk and she felt that if she tried to move she would lose her balance. She felt dizzy, breathless.

'She was the logical choice,' he said wryly. 'I liked her and we had a lot in common. But love...' He shook his head. 'When she and Juan had their battle royal, when he stormed off and left her crying all over the excavation south of Mérida——' He shrugged. 'I sent Juan a cable. It wasn't hard to figure out what would bring him back. The suggestion that if he didn't get back into her life I'd do what I could to take his woman.'

Juan's woman. There was no regret in Ricardo's eyes as he acknowledged Juan Corsica's right to his wife.

'Juan said he owes you,' whispered Maria. 'Is that what he meant? Because you gave him Cathy?'

'Maria, do you imagine that if you wanted another man, I'd help you win him?' She saw a shudder go through him. She could see the fire in his eyes. She released her grip on the desk behind her and lifted her head high.

'No.' She gulped and whispered, 'I'm such a coward,' and her eyelashes fluttered down to hide her fears.

He touched her. 'Tell me what you want,' he demanded. She opened her eyes and something in his gaze caught her heart. The look in his eyes was like the tenderness in his voice when he had given her one last chance to run before he became her lover.

'Ricardo...I couldn't bear it if I never saw you again.'

'You'll see me.' He stroked her upper arms slowly. 'You're recording in Mexico City next week. I'll be there at the studio. I've been invited as Señor Descanso's guest. I arranged it the day after I saw you on the television.'

'I——' She felt colour flood into her face. 'I looked for a rose when I came off stage in Mexico City. I looked for your rose and when it wasn't there——' She bit her lip and blinked and mercifully no tears came.

'You sent me away,' he reminded her. 'You said you didn't want me in your life.'

'I was afraid.' She drew in a deep breath. 'Afraid of what you made me feel. Afraid I was all wrong for you and that if you—if we—you'd regret it and I'd always have to see you wishing I were different.'

She turned away from the look in his eyes. A question and she didn't know his answer to the question she could not ask. She was at the window and he was behind her. Better this way, her face averted from him.

'I'm not trying to force you into anything.' His voice was reasonable, quiet. It was not the voice that would tell her what was in his heart. 'I should never have tried to force you—to pressure you——'

She spun around. 'I chose to be your lover!'

'I know that, *querida*. But marriage—you never chose that, did you?'

'Why?' she asked shakily. 'Why did you pressure me towards marriage?'

'What is it you want with me now?' he countered.

She turned away. She wanted to go through the glass door in front of her, to run out on the beach. He would follow her and it would be so much easier if they could lose this tension in the storm of their loving.

'What can I have?' she asked.

'Are you fencing with me?'

She shrugged her shoulders. 'We both are, aren't we?'

'Why?'

'I don't know why you are.' She sighed. 'I'm afraid. I came to tell you...but I'm afraid you won't want...that I——' She clenched her hands into fists. 'Damn!' she whispered passionately. '*Maldición*!'

'Maria...'

His hands were on her shoulders from behind. He pulled her back and she melted against him, the strength of his chest against her back and her shoulders caught in the slow caress of his fingers on them. She closed her eyes and the dizziness took her so that her weight rested against him and she would have fallen if he had moved away.

'What did you come to tell me?'

She rolled her head against his chest in protest. 'Will you take everything from me?' she whispered.

'I want to give you everything.' His voice was husky, trembling. His mouth against her hair. 'From the first moment I saw you I was lost.'

'The gypsy. On stage.' She closed her eyes and hoped the tears would not begin to flow. He'd wanted the gypsy from the beginning.

'I told myself it was the gypsy. God, darling, I needed you so desperately, I had to tell myself something! Anything was better—any lie to myself was better than the truth!' He turned her in his arms and she was staring up into his face and the question was on her lips.

'Tell me the truth now.'

'I took one look at you and I was lost. No matter how long I live, my gypsy, if I am without you I shall wake every morning in emptiness and lie every night alone aching for my love.'

She caught her bottom lip between her teeth and he shook his head, using the side of his thumb to break the pain of her teeth against her own flesh.

'Ricardo, I——'

He shook his head and covered her lips with his thumb. 'No, *querida*, I must tell you this. You intrigued me at first and I told myself it was that alone. That I would penetrate your mystery. But when I discovered a vulnerable, frightened woman under the mask, I—I was already lost. Even though you feared the act of love, I saw in your eyes that you felt the same need I felt. I knew that I could overcome your fears if only I had enough time. But it was wrong of me to take what you gave—to take your sweet sensual innocence and your trust——' His voice broke and she felt his hands tighten on her arms. 'To take that from you and not give you the truth.'

'The truth?' She was frightened. His eyes were tender on her and his hands moving gently. Soon the tenderness would burn into passion and she could feel her own flesh aching for that moment. But first he would tell her the truth.

He took her face in his hands and whispered, 'When you came to me today I hoped you would tell me that you were carrying our child. I wanted——' He shook his head. 'What else could we do then but marry? I know what you said the day you sent me away, but you would marry me for the child. I know it would be wrong, and I promise you I won't again try to make you give me a part of yourself that you fear to share, but——' He dragged in a harsh breath and confessed, 'I will take whatever you will give me of yourself. If you want me to be your lover, to meet you in whatever city we can meet, then I will be your lover. If you want—if you want only a friend, then—even that would be better than this! Not knowing where you are and what you are doing! Wishing—aching to know you are near.'

She touched his face and felt a muscle in his cheek spasm in response. 'You love me,' she whispered. 'You do love me?' She saw it in his eyes and felt the trembling in his body and wondered how she could not have known. He'd said she could find the true emotion in him and it was true. From that first dance when she'd flamed into defensive anger.

'Yes,' he said, and his voice was harsh. 'I love you. I think I have always loved you.'

She melted against him and he took her body in his arms. She closed her eyes and sought his mouth with hers and when the kiss came it burned through her from her centre outwards and left her trembling. He swung her into his arms and she let her head rest against his shoulder.

'I came to tell you I love you,' she whispered. She found the button of his shirt and opened it so that she could press her mouth against his chest. He was carrying her and she could feel the hammer of his heart against her cheek. 'You haven't shown me the bedroom yet,' she breathed.

'I love you.' He said it harshly as he lowered her on to the softness. Not the bed but a soft sofa that took her weight gently. He cradled her face and she saw the love in his eyes and he said, 'And I am going to love you as I have dreamed all the days and nights since I was with you.' His mouth was buried in hers and she pressed herself against him with all the passion pounding in her pulse, so that he was trembling when he broke away from her.

'Tell me what you want, *querida*.' His fingers trembled as he worked his way down the buttons of her bodice. Then he pushed the sides apart and there was only a lacy bra with a single front-closing between his touch and the aching flush of her breasts. 'I'll give you anything you ask...the moon...the stars...all the roses in the world.'

'Love me,' she begged, and he slowly drew the fabric barriers away from her so that there was only the heated fire burning on her flesh and the hard masculine drive of his. Then he broke away from her and she stared up and saw his eyes haunted and dark. She put her fingers over his mouth and felt the pressure of his kiss on her hand.

'Ricardo,' she whispered. 'I wanted your child. When I realised it hadn't happened—I cried. And when I danced in Mexico City——' She shook her head and thought she could not tell him, but there was nothing stopping the words now and they came. 'When the performance was over that first night—the night it was televised—when it was over and the music was silent I knew that was the real truth. The gypsy standing alone with the music gone and knowing you were not there watching. I would be alone all my life aching for the loving you'd offered me—because I was too much of a coward to reach for what I wanted.'

His hands threaded into her hair and his mouth took hers and she gave him everything that was in her heart, and he kissed her back so that she had no doubt she was the only woman he had ever wanted with this depth of love and passion.

'There's only one thing,' he said, and his voice was thick with emotion so that tears flooded into her eyes. '*Querida . . . Maria, mi amante.*'

'*Sí?*'

He stroked her body slowly with his hands. Caressed the slope of her breast and left her gasping as his fingers traced the curve of her waist, the woman's flare of her hip.

'Do you still want my child?' His eyes asked a deeper question.

'I want everything. I want . . . you . . . *querido* . . . forever.' She touched him boldly and saw his eyes darken beyond black.

'You'll marry me?'

She smiled then. 'Oh, yes! You will have to marry me now. I am a traditional girl, you know. You may be a modern *norte americano*, but——'

'Not that modern,' he growled. 'I want your ring on my finger and mine on yours. And when you stand up there and sing so that any sane man would die to possess you, I want the world to know that you are my wife . . . only mine.'

'Yes,' she promised. 'Only yours.' She smiled, and a small voice reminded her that she had fantasied that he might still want her as his wife. And in her fantasy she had needed to know all the crazy unimportant things, like where they would live and whether her singing would be a part of her that he would want changed.

But she understood now that only this mattered: their love for each other. She knew only a few details about her lover, but she understood finally that he loved her and she trusted him to cherish her and to love her truly enough that he would not ask her to change into a person she could not be.

And she flowed deeply into his embrace and showed him how much he was her lover, and how their loving would be through all the days of their marriage. When he tensed in her arms she welcomed his need, and her own passion burned hot and wild so that she cried out his name and heard him vow his love forever as the dark, heated waves of their mutual seduction overcame the world around.

# Accept 4 FREE Romances and 2 FREE gifts

## FROM READER SERVICE

Here's an irresistible invitation from Mills & Boon. Please accept our offer of 4 FREE Romances, a CUDDLY TEDDY and a special MYSTERY GIFT! Then, if you choose, go on to enjoy 6 captivating Romances every month for just £1.80 each, postage and packing FREE. Plus our FREE Newsletter with author news, competitions and much more.

**Send the coupon below to:**
**Mills & Boon Reader Service,**
**FREEPOST, PO Box 236,**
**Croydon, Surrey CR9 9EL.**

---

**NO STAMP REQUIRED**

## Yes! Please rush me 4 FREE Romances and 2 FREE gifts!

Please also reserve me a Reader Service subscription. If I decide to subscribe I can look forward to receiving 6 brand new Romances for just £10.80 each month, post and packing FREE. If I decide not to subscribe I shall write to you within 10 days - I can keep the free books and gifts whatever I choose. I may cancel or suspend my subscription at any time. I am over 18 years of age.

Ms/Mrs/Miss/Mr _____ EP55R

Address _____

_____

Postcode _____ Signature _____

mps
MAILING PREFERENCE SERVICE

# Next Month's Romances

Each month you can choose from a wide variety of romance with Mills & Boon. Below are the new titles to look out for next month, why not ask either Mills & Boon Reader Service or your Newsagent to reserve you a copy of the titles you want to buy – just tick the titles you would like and either post to Reader Service or take it to any Newsagent and ask them to order your books.

| *Please save me the following titles:* | | Please tick √ |
|---|---|---|
| **HEART-THROB FOR HIRE** | Miranda Lee | |
| **A SECRET REBELLION** | Anne Mather | |
| **THE CRUELLEST LIE** | Susan Napier | |
| **THE AWAKENED HEART** | Betty Neels | |
| **ITALIAN INVADER** | Jessica Steele | |
| **A RECKLESS ATTRACTION** | Kay Thorpe | |
| **BITTER HONEY** | Helen Brooks | |
| **THE POWER OF LOVE** | Rosemary Hammond | |
| **MASTER OF DECEIT** | Susanne McCarthy | |
| **THE TOUCH OF APHRODITE** | Joanna Mansell | |
| **POSSESSED BY LOVE** | Natalie Fox | |
| **GOLDEN MISTRESS** | Angela Wells | |
| **NOT FOR LOVE** | Pamela Hatton | |
| **SHATTERED MIRROR** | Kate Walker | |
| **A MOST CONVENIENT MARRIAGE** | Suzanne Carey | |
| **TEMPORARY MEASURES** | Leigh Michaels | |

If you would like to order these books in addition to your regular subscription from Mills & Boon Reader Service please send £1.80 per title to: Mills & Boon Reader Service, Freepost, P.O. Box 236, Croydon, Surrey, CR9 9EL, quote your Subscriber No:.................................... (If applicable) and complete the name and address details below. Alternatively, these books are available from many local Newsagents including W.H.Smith, J.Menzies, Martins and other paperback stockists from 11 February 1994.

Name:.............................................................................

Address:..........................................................................

..............................................................Post Code:...........................

**To Retailer: If you would like to stock M&B books please contact your regular book/magazine wholesaler for details.**

You may be mailed with offers from other reputable companies as a result of this application. If you would rather not take advantage of these opportunities please tick box ☐